TIMON'S TIDE

CHARLES BUTLER

A Dolphin
Paperback

First published in Great Britain in 1998
as a Dolphin paperback
by Orion Children's Books
a division of the Orion Publishing Group Ltd
Orion House
5 Upper St Martin's Lane
London WC2H 9EA

A catalogue record for this book
is available from the British Library

Printed in Great Britain

ISBN 1 85881 646 7

To my children:
Cecily, Nathaniel and Charlotte

One

*A*BOVE THE LONG RIBS OF SAND THE MOON winked: a banner flying out from the wharf had flapped across it. There were so few lights on the river, so many dark windows, and the tide was out. The sand-ribs were spread with their own granular moonlight, and pools of water, molasses-thick. You could smell the sea. Half a mile away the cranes reared high above the dock.

'I don't want to drown,' said Timon.

Five minutes' walk from here (if your legs were free for walking) people could be found in bars and bistros, and all the harlequin lights glittered. Voices spoke of wine and money. A taxi cruised for fares. Good times. Others begged from blankets, and their thin dogs scratched. But it was no use shouting.

'I don't want to drown. Kill me first, if you have to.'

'Perhaps you won't drown. The rats may oblige you.'

They worked hard with stakes and mallets. Three men, one hardly more than a boy. Plastic cords bound wrist and ankle. No one spoke after that.

At length the eldest stood for breath. He tugged the last stake and found it firm, then squatted beside the youth spread-eagled on the sand.

'The stars are out.'

'I've learnt my lesson. Let me go. *Please.*'

'But you're missing the point, Timon. You *are* the lesson – see?'

A length of tape stopped Timon's mouth. The man patted him on the cheek, then, with a salt-damp palm. 'You take care now. Be good.'

He turned to go, all weary, and tramped over the sand. The others followed.

'Be careful – don't lie too long!'

'Tide's turning!'

'Goodbye, Timon.'

They shambled off, departing revellers. The daring of it all had made them a bit drunk. In the morning they would spew out the horror, and sit with shaking limbs in front of the television, thinking of what they had done, waiting for news. When someone knocked at the door they would jump. They would not sleep. All except the eldest, and he would be thinking it was a pity, sure, how it was always the smart ones who tried to break the rules. But it passed off well enough, he would say. And Timon March won't be taking him for a fool again.

That was one way of imagining it. There were others, other ways of writing Timon's name in the dust. Daniel knew them all. He had lived and died them: felt the cold water lap his heels, the rats' scuttering feet. Timon had played a dangerous game and lost. But just what had he done, whom had he offended? There were answers to these questions, too many to sort out, and Daniel did not know how. Six years ago the tide had sluiced away his brother's body, pulling stakes from the sandbank like pins. By difficult currents it had been carried out to sea, and landed a good two miles away on a rocky beach. And there imagination lost its grip, for that story – of police, inquests, reports – belonged to other people, and in a thousand official forms they had told it. Timon's life was over. That was the point.

Daniel slid out of bed. He couldn't lie there any longer: he was getting afraid of the stillness, and what sleep might bring. It was now just four-thirty. His cold nose prophesied a chill. He dressed quickly, two jumpers and Max's old waxed jacket. One finger slid the length of the banisters. The mood still clung to him as he descended. Something to do with water, and broken surfaces.

In the dining-room everything lay as it had the night before, the remains of his mother's and Max's party. Plates were piled at the side, wine glasses paddling in blue candle wax. He saw the bottles, three or four of them – the wine that made Max so talkative, and more so last night than usual. Last night, and something Max had said, teased at his brain. Later the cigarette smoke would bring on one of Ruby's air-freshening crusades, with windows open and a horizontal breeze. Daniel made a sandwich from yesterday's cold joint, and went to the garage for the fishing gear. He filled a plastic box from a writhing bucket of live bait, fed on some concoction best not pried into. The canal was just beyond the woods.

The closing of the door woke his mother, Lisa. 'What was that? Max, did you hear?'

Max grunted, snored, and started drifting again. 'Uh?'

'The door. I heard it close. Do you think someone's come into the house?'

He raised himself on his elbow. 'Or gone out. Doors have that dual function.'

'At this time of day? Night, I mean! It's pitch black.'

'Daniel has gone hunter-gathering I expect, my love. He'll be down on the canal with rod and line.'

Lisa had to admit this was likely: Daniel often went. 'But what if someone's breaking in?' she persisted after half a minute. 'Don't you think you'd better check?'

Max's head wasn't too good. He didn't fancy a wild goose chase, thanks – creeping around in the dark with a poker. Always supposing it *was* a wild goose chase. And if not – well! Even less appealing. The hi-fi was insured, come to that. He changed the subject. 'There's only one intruder in this house,' he said, rubbing his wife's abdomen. He caressed it with his fingers, whispering in her ear: 'And he's not going anywhere for the next few months.'

'He?' she asked, prepared to be soothed this way.

'My intuition.'

'Mmm.'

He looked down at her in the dim starlight, thinking, 'I'm going to be a father again. After everything.' Though he had no intention of leaving his bed, Lisa's appeal had made him feel chivalrous and protective. 'It's hard to believe,' he said.

'I know,' she replied softly – it was exciting to think they might be overheard. 'I think it will be that way as long as it's a secret. Like our private game.'

He hesitated. 'When do you think we should speak to the children?'

'Soon. Not just yet. I mean, Ruby's bound to be upset, and Daniel …' Lisa wasn't sure how to put this. 'To have a new brother or sister, and so unexpected – it won't be easy.'

'They may surprise you. It won't get easier for waiting.'

'No, it won't. But let's have this time to ourselves

first, Max. There'll be no other. Not for years and years and years.'

He kissed her, as her voice faded. 'You are a wise old bird, Lisa.'

'I know,' said Lisa, and promptly fell asleep.

An hour later Ruby was disturbed by the coughing from Aunt Jenkins' room. Despite everything Aunt Jenkins smoked in bed, and one day, Ruby was sure, she would incinerate herself and half the house, and Max would regret not fitting a smoke alarm, and Ruby would point out how often she had asked him. But what would be the good of that?

Soon she was making tea, watching her hands go through the ritual of warming the pot, counting out the spoonfuls, and enjoying the regularity of that start to every day. But she screwed her face up at the smell of cigarette smoke.

By rising early Ruby gained a precious hour on her father's computer. The PC was her excuse, but the main attraction was the study itself: a windowless white-walled box, good for concentrating in. Max called it his asylum-for-one. Tea first, though. Her knock was answered by Aunt Jenkins' cracked cough of thanks. Ruby slipped the cup onto the table by the door without entering. For her father and Lisa, a tray on the carpet outside their room. The radio alarm was already provoking sounds of reluctant movement from their iron bedstead. Ruby wondered how much Lisa would be able to keep down this morning.

A year almost to the day since Max had moved her to this old mongrel house, and Ruby still could not get used to it. Its carpets and odd jutting walls conspired to knock her elbow, trip her feet. She could never remember where the light switches were, and found herself fumbling the wall. In one alcove on the landing it seemed to her a door ought to have been: every day she was surprised at finding it bare plaster still. The Easter vacation had barely begun, but already she longed for her Hall of Residence, with all its predictable modern dinginess.

Ruby closed the study door behind her, feeling the wood swish snugly against the new carpet. The place felt secure at last, and she settled down to her psychology revision. The morning would be devoted to the libido, with psychosis pencilled in for the afternoon. Ruby's head was awash with facts. Absorbed, she did not see the time, and (because the study had no windows) she did not see how dawn had crept up on this raggedly-begun day, or how the wind had sucked the blossom from the cherry trees and sent it in a pink torrent past the kitchen. Or how dismal the sky was. By now Aunt Jenkins had padded down for her second cup of Earl Grey, and was muttering that winter had come again.

The fields were still in ruins from the spring storms. It was like that all the way to the coast. Last week the sea had overwhelmed the breakwaters, snapping the marina masts like daffodil stems. Where the city ran into the marshes people had been forced to climb roofs, or become bath-tub gondoliers. For two days the wind came howling – 'With the voice of Leviathan,' as Aunt Jenkins put it. Some tried to reassure themselves with talk of cyclonic fronts and charts, but when they heard the wind rattle their doors or the explosion of a chimney pot on the slabs outside, they were afraid. Until at last the tide seethed back over black shingle, and the salt wind swept on to season inland soil.

First light found Daniel sheltered in a hollow, watching the grasses on the far bank flatten. A water rat had made him look up, a flock of geese. One fish swam back and forth, slapping against the keepnet. Gradually Daniel had achieved a perilous calm: thought about Timon less, and Jane Garfield more, and wished she was sitting beside him. He looked along the line of twisted fencing leading the canal down to the city. What if Jane came walking along the towpath now? What would he say?

If Timon were alive he could advise him, as elder brothers do. Daniel loved Jane Garfield. Love of her drew him to think about the future: that must be good. But perhaps they did not have a future. One awkward kiss sealed nothing. One kiss – and that was in the past, a cut flower fading. The way she looked at Gabriel Spicer sometimes made him doubt. She had promised nothing. And was he worth a promise?

Daniel tossed a handful of bait onto the water, and rubbed his fingers. If Timon were here he would advise him, perhaps. But Timon's advice might not be good to take. Timon's idea of a fast buck had got him killed. Why should he be luckier in love?

Timon had been seventeen when he died. Soon Daniel would overtake him. But still his brother seemed aloof, a source of untappable adult power and knowledge. And somehow Daniel was still that trailing child, the Velcro Kid, Timon's willing gopher. Nothing had changed, though everything was different. He ran the treadmill of the last few years in his mind. How Lisa had given up the band, and Valentine, his father, taken off at last. Then Timon's death, and the frenetic, empty time that followed – until Max, a widower with a daughter, came to settle on their lives. There must have been something Daniel could have done to make it better …

There were a thousand things.

Coming home he looked in at the kitchen window. They were all sitting round the table, his family. Aunt Jenkins first, fanning herself with a copy of the *Daily Mail*. If she looked up now she would jerk back in surprise with a 'Saints preserve us!' at the sight of his face against the glass, all streaked with dirt. Aunt Jenkins was easy to predict. And so were the rest. Lisa, capable and wise-cracking like a sitcom Mum, getting it all done. Ruby playing Ruby, with her cherry smile and Ryvita waist. And Max, a bit hazy round the edges this time of day, charmingly bathrobed at the table's head. A Dad to poke fun at: but always loving fun, mind, because a heart of gold was said to lurk thereabouts.

Daniel had one carp to show for his efforts. Max would work it out. 'Three hours for one fish, price in the fishmongers, three pounds. You've been working for a pound an hour, Daniel! And unsocial hours too!' Lisa would not help. And Ruby would say: 'But you do it for the fun, don't you Daniel?' Or perhaps: 'I don't approve of bloodsports.' That was the trouble with Ruby. You could never tell which way she'd jump.

It would not be forgotten by anyone that all Daniel's gear – the rod, waders, keepnet and the rest – had once been Max's. Still were, strictly speaking (though Max never did speak strictly to his stepson). And this made Daniel want to turn back to the canal, numb his hands in the black water there, and feel nothing.

Aunt Jenkins left half the cup – and when she opened her eyes the tea was cold. Everyone had gone, and she was alone. She did not think about how Max and Lisa had their work to go to, Ruby the library, Daniel school. She knew all that, but the important thing was: they had left her alone, and the tea was cold, and before that it had been tasteless, like it always was these days. She would talk to Lisa about it. Her Tolly now – there was a man who knew how to make a proper brew.

Daniel was the image of Tolly, had Tolly lived to see it. How proud he would have been! But Timon had had Tolly's eyes, all yellowy gold; and Lisa his chin. So Tolly was shared out, after all. That was fair.

It was past ten, and she still in her dressing-gown. It would never do. What would – what would *anyone* think, seeing her there? But of course no one would see her. There was no one to call her a lazy thing, now. No one expected anything. Oh, this tea! She poured the lot straight down the sink, and blocked it. And another thing. That young man nosing round the house, there was a thing. Several times she'd seen him from the corner of her eye. Max should call the police. Staring in people's windows – and she still in her dressing-gown. They could all be murdered in their beds, and no one the wiser.

The knocking at the back door roused her. Aware of the state she was in, Aunt Jenkins wondered if she should go up to her room to change; but there was no time, and she could not face the stairs. She unbolted the door.

'Hello,' she said, surprised. 'I didn't expect *you* home today. I'm not sure you should be here at all. Well come in, come in now you're here, you'll catch your death.'

She turned about, all of a bustle, and put the kettle on again. She told her visitor to sit, to wipe the mud from his boots. Such a surprise! And she still in her dressing-gown. It would never do.

But when she looked back, the door was swinging open, the first specks of rain were gusting onto her bare legs, and she was alone. In the highest trees the wind was shaking out a confession. And Tolly Jenkins' wife sat down and nibbled at a biscuit, and wondered how – if she had not imagined it completely – any relative of hers could be so rude.

Two

LISA MIGHT HAVE DROPPED DANIEL ON HER WAY to the solicitor's, but he preferred to go to school on foot. At the age of eleven the decision to tramp four miles a day had been a bid for independence: only little kids got taken to school by their mums. Five years on, the reasons had fanned out and become complicated, harder to put into words but just as final. Each day he bore the lazy mockery of the churchyard rooks; had his teeth set on edge by the pylons' buzzing. Then there was the chance of foxes nearer town – lean foxes scavenging in yards and shop backs. Sometimes they would watch him, too. He felt their eyes.

Home was no longer a refuge, not with Max and Ruby there. The house was full of their things, still half-packed. Most would never leave the crates: the metal and blue-painted pine of Max's dockside flat would never settle. In due course, when Max could bear to part with them, they would be auctioned off or dumped. The house asserted itself subtly; but it was not Daniel's home any longer, and never could be. School was little better. Gabriel Spicer had become his enemy the day Jane had first talked to him. The sight of Jane herself still set his heart beating like a rabbit's. School was impossible. But the walk between was his.

He thought about the dinner party. Max's voice had

been locked into a high and flashy gear last night, the way it always was by the second bottle of wine. If he *talked* about the wine, that was a bad sign. He liked to show off, but was usually restrained – by a fear of being too obvious. By the second bottle he forgot not to be obvious. Daniel had heard about the wine, and then the needle which always came Lisa's way when she discussed something she knew more about than him. Conveyancing it was this time – as if anyone would *want* to know. Then those friends of hers had steered the subject round to a man they'd all met and Max hadn't, which made things worse. The police patholo-gist. Max was snapping like a terrier at the edges of the conversation, getting nowhere. You'd need to be a bit sick, he said, to enjoy examining bodies. Doctors were there to make people well. And then, from that fruit pudding of a brain, he had pulled out such a ripe and juicy plum …

Timon's body had lain on the shingle. A dog had found him. The owner had mistaken him at first for a piece of driftwood, but that was from the far end of the beach. When he got closer there was no mistaking. Daniel had known all that – was it from newspapers? He couldn't remember. But Max had known some-thing else again.

A lorry overtook him on the lane. A cat leaping from the roadside ditch made it swerve a little. Houses were beginning to peep from behind the trees. Daniel followed the footpath between and beyond them till he met the canal again, and crossed it at a lock. The iron water gleamed beneath him, while on the far side of the gates the patient tons pressed silently.

Inside his pocket he fingered the postcard from Jane Garfield that had become his talisman. Later that morning she would be set against him in an end-of-term balloon debate organised by the science teacher, Mr Marx: Louis Pasteur versus Archimedes. It was odd, but before Christmas Jane had meant no more to him than a dozen other girls in his class. Fun to pass time with, but too clannish, given to bouts of suppressed giggling with her friend Meg Aitken. Anyone who'd gone out with Gabriel had to be missing *something*. It was hard to remember those days. The party before Christmas had changed everything. It was then that Jane had found him at a loss and led him outside, and kissed him. To show how it was done.

'Move your nose aside, you funny thing!'

'It's not on hinges you know.'

She thought he was funny. He made the class laugh out loud, even Mrs Lockwood. She laughed now, and with her lips apart pressed them onto his.

'Was that nice?'

Daniel could hardly breathe.

'Was it nice?'

'Oh yes.' The taste of her breath. 'It was nice.'

'Merry Christmas.' Again she kissed him, but this time it was on the tip of that awkward nose, and not romantic. She glanced back at the light from the school hall. The dance was pulling her away like a ghost at cock-crow.

'Will I see you?' Daniel asked. 'Can I phone you?'

'I'm going away – we're spending Christmas at my gran's.'

'When will you be back?'

'I'll write to you, OK?' Jane smiled. 'Don't look so worried! I like you, all right?'

How pathetic he must have looked, to need that! But he was grateful. He murmured something, and soon after stumbled home, though his feet were no longer attached to his legs. He had never been kissed before.

The first week of the Christmas holidays had been spent playing reruns of that kiss in his memory – until at last the film grew grainy and unsure. The ache had begun by then, which had blotted out everything. Jane had not written. She had said she would, but she hadn't. The huge fact beached itself at the centre of his life. Nothing was reliable, not even the kiss itself. The thrill of it was a tasteless, overchewed morsel. He wondered why she'd looked at him at all. Something to do with the cider on her breath, perhaps. 'I like you,' she had told him. Like, not love: the verb was ominous.

In fact a card had arrived in early January, with a picture of a goat and five pink kisses. Briefly he'd allowed himself to hope. But that was weeks ago, and the pink kisses had not been converted into real ones. At school Jane talked to him, but no more than to other boys. Several of them had received postcards too, he discovered. For a while he wondered if she was just waiting for the right time ... But there would be no right time. She liked him, but did not want him. She wished him to be happy, but not with her. Whenever he tried to get her alone, half a dozen of her friends appeared by magic, and all the intimate, perfect things he had been going to say became impossible. He'd been a fool, and that was that.

Now he was in a housing estate. Each house here had a name – Bellevue, Deauville, Squirrel's Leap – and a picketed garden, and a tree. Daniel quickened his pace slightly. At the shop he bought crisps for break, and sealed them in his lunch-box. School was on the edge of this rich estate: he did not have to penetrate the city. As he left the shop he looked back up the street, to mock-tudor Deauville. Something was moving. A fox was standing just beside the fence; or had just withdrawn behind it. The impression was strong, of red fur, speed, of caution, of eyes like yellow gaslight. And a *smell*. Though Daniel had seen nothing but a flicker of movement, all this was vividly with him.

It must have been a fox.

He reached the school – and there his heart betrayed him. Jane was just inside the gates. Her long hair was straggled by the wind. Her skirt was pasted to her legs on one side, a fluttering pennant beyond. She was talking to Meg Aitken and a couple of Meg's cronies. All four teetered forward in a walk that hardly differed from standing, but gradually they wheeled round and disappeared into the chemistry block. As she stepped inside Jane looked in his direction, and smiled right at him. The playground stood empty. Daniel glanced at his watch, and saw that he was late.

He'd been a fool, he thought fiercely. To waste time on a girl who no more thought of him than …

But it made no difference. Jane's smile had sunk him. He was still her fool, with cap and bells and all.

An hour later Archimedes, Isaac Newton, Louis Pasteur and Einstein were floating half a mile above a rocky plain. The balloon in which they were travelling had jettisoned its sandbags. Various possessions followed: apples, test tubes, spectacles, syringes and a toga. It was no good, they were still descending, and fast. They needed to lose more weight. Hurried calculations revealed that one man might survive, where four would surely perish. But who was to make the sacrifice?

Perhaps no one took it quite as seriously as Mr

Marx, who planned it, but the whole class was a little tense, and quieter than usual – except for Gabriel and his friends. They acted up from the start.

'The idea of a balloon debate,' Mr Marx announced, 'is to justify your continued existence. Have you saved lives? Have you discovered a fundamental law of nature? What makes you a better candidate than your fellow travellers?'

Mr Marx's eyes fairly shone. He believed in what he was teaching, and the way he was teaching it. And it was true (Daniel had to admit it), he had a gift. Jane, for one, had worked harder to prepare herself for five minutes as Louis Pasteur (even developing a slight French accent) than she ever had at learning the periodic table for Mrs Lockwood the previous term. The details of the rabies cure seemed suddenly fascinating. Perhaps Jane was a bit in love with Mr Marx. Meg Aitken teased her about it, and Jane blushed and told her to mind her own business, but not that she was wrong. So that was proof. Mr Marx was not good-looking, exactly – there was even a slight paunch visible on his sweaterless days, Daniel noted. It was his *enthusiasm*. Whatever he did, he did it whole. Enthusiasm. Oh dear – and that was just what Daniel lacked. Jane was watching him now, as gloomy an Archimedes as ever plummeted from a hot-air balloon.

'In 212 BC I kept the Romans out of Syracuse for several months, designing catapults and other engines of war to defeat the siege. But perhaps mankind is most indebted to me for my invention of the water screw.'

'Water screw? What's that then?'

'Something you do in a water bed!'

'Gabriel, Duncan – that's enough! Daniel has worked hard on this. Let's give him a chance.'

Mr Marx meant it. But somehow Daniel did not feel grateful.

'Sorry, sir. Don't know what came over me.' Tall, straight-backed, with blond hair cropped short, Gabriel Spicer stared blankly forward, like a soldier up on a charge. He kept a straight face, eyes straight ahead. Dead straight. Not meeting your gaze, not avoiding it – a kind of alert trance. 'It won't happen again.'

Everyone knew he was cheeking Mr Marx.

'Carry on, Daniel.'

'This simple device allowed water to be raised from an underground source by the application of horizontal pressure, for example by a pair of yoked oxen ...'

Daniel had copied it straight from a book. The class began to fidget. It was a relief when, as he reached the end of his speech, something sharp hit Daniel in the back of the neck. He winced and sat down. A biro fell on the floor beside him.

'I resign sir,' Daniel said. 'Archimedes is dead.'

'Gabriel!'

'Yes, sir?'

'Stand up.'

Gabriel Spicer lumbered to his feet. He was taller than Mr Marx.

'Where's your pen?'

Gabriel searched ostentatiously for his pen, patting his pockets and lifting exercise books. 'I don't seem to have it on me, sir. I must have left it at home.'

'Really?'

'Yes, I remember now. On the mantelpiece, next to my parents' wedding photograph. I can bring it in next time.'

'That won't be necessary. Daniel, give Gabriel his

— 17 —

pen back.' Daniel returned it. Gabriel's palm was open, and he dropped it in without touching.

'Thank you, sir,' said Gabriel. 'That's a life-saver. Your sharp eyes. Where would I be without my pen?'

'Gabriel?'

'Yes, sir?'

'Shut up.'

'Glad to, sir.'

'And Gabriel' – Mr Marx couldn't quite let it go at that – 'don't get clever with me, son. I've seen it all before.'

But no doubt Gabriel had got the best of it. With a cough of frustration Mr Marx called Albert Einstein to the stand.

'You were pathetic, March,' said Gabriel Spicer, when he and Daniel found themselves squeezing through the chemistry block door together after the bell.

Daniel didn't seem to hear. But Jane said, 'I suppose you think *you* looked pretty wonderful.'

'I wasn't talking about me.'

'"Yes, sir, no sir, three bags of bull, sir,"' said Jane.

'At least I didn't copy out the *Encyclopaedia Britannica*. Daniel has got no idea. You don't know when to stop, do you Daniel?'

Daniel carried on walking.

'I'm talking to you, Danny boy!' Gabriel kicked the playground gate shut before Daniel got to it. It hit the frame and juddered a few inches. 'You deaf?'

Daniel turned slowly. The world was looking strange, as it had all day, the sky a little darker, redder. Usually Gabriel Spicer frightened him, but now he seemed unreal too. Like Mr Marx's hot air, and the hot-air balloon. Gabriel, moving closer, felt further away: a tiny gnome, shaking a toothpick spear on the horizon. 'You have a problem?'

'Not me, March. I'm not the one with the problem.'

Only give me a firm spot on which to stand, Archimedes had said, and I will move the world. Daniel had been going to finish with that – a tribute to the power of the lever. Now it occurred to him that the world was moving anyway. 'You bore me,' he said, and waited to see what would happen.

Nothing, because Jane stepped in. 'We're already late for English. Give it a rest, will you?'

'Look at those two turkey cocks, ruffling up their feathers!' Meg Aitken squawked and flapped her elbows. 'You'd almost think they were human.' Some of the girls laughed.

Gabriel Spicer's blue eyes were locked on Daniel's. His nose was so close Daniel could hear it snuffling – Gabriel was getting over a cold. They must have looked silly.

'I wouldn't waste my breath on a March,' said Gabriel. 'It's in the blood.'

'What do you mean?' said Jane.

'Losers, they are,' he said turning away. 'Or worse.'

The gnome was waving his tooth-pick spear. Daniel felt nothing. 'Tell me, Gabriel. You know so much.'

'Everyone knows about your brother, Daniel. He didn't get that way without a reason.'

'What way?'

Gabriel looked at him. 'Fish bait.'

'Gabriel!' Jane hissed.

'What's wrong? Swallowed your tongue?'

'Leave him alone, Spicer,' someone said.

'Look at him,' said Gabriel, lips opening into a smile. 'He's going to cry.'

— 19 —

Daniel wouldn't cry for Spicer. He was wondering what would happen if he hit him. Surprise was worth a lot – but would it make up for Gabriel Spicer's reach? And those muscles?

'You're going to cry, aren't you March? I can see the tears coming!'

Gabriel bent forward, peering into Daniel's face. His big flat nose snuffled some more. With an intake of breath, Daniel drew back his arm and punched it hard.

'It's all guesswork with him. He uses words to hurt because he's scared to use his fists.'

Jane had found Daniel under the stairs, on one of the benches beside the coat hooks. Daniel had been trying to engineer a moment alone with her for weeks, and now he couldn't bring himself to speak.

'He shouldn't have brought Timon into it.'

'No.'

'I'd have beaten him, you know.'

'I think you would, too, the way you were going. Lucky Mr Marx came along.'

Three or four younger children charged down the iron stairwell above their heads.

'Daniel.'

Doors banged, and the children's voices fell away.

'Daniel, what's wrong?'

Daniel was shivering, hands clasped between his knees.

'You shouldn't take any notice of him, Daniel. I know him. He'll have forgotten all about it by now. Why do you think I—'

'It's not Gabriel. Will you stop going on about him?'

Jane was taking a good look at him, the dirt under his fingernails. Pity – had she ever felt more than that for him? His hair needed cutting too: it had lost all sense of purpose round the collar. 'What is it then?' she asked.

Daniel could not very well say. There *were* reasons for the way he felt now. They were swimming round and through him, lurking like carp among the weeds. But the water was murky. Now and then a fishy mouth would break the surface and gulp.

'He didn't have much of a face left.'

'What?'

'When they found him. Timon – his face had been eaten away.'

Jane took a moment to catch up. When she did, she gasped. 'That's awful!'

Daniel shrugged. 'Fish bait. It made no difference to him, not if he was dead already.' Daniel did not quite hit the note he was after. He wasn't sure whether Timon had been dead.

'What – how do they think it happened?'

'Max didn't go into details. I overheard what I wasn't meant to last night. They never *tell* me anything.' He tried to explain about Max and Lisa's parties. 'When there's six people all talking at once, you don't get high fidelity. They were comparing books, and TV programmes they'd seen, and Max was saying how sometimes you could identify a body by the teeth. Then they got on to DNA testing, and how clever it all was. And they talked about Timon's face ...'

Daniel realised that Jane was close beside him, her arm across his back.

'That's gross. In front of your mum, too.'

'He waited till Mum was in the kitchen before he got started. He's a cunning drunk.'

'I wouldn't put up with it, if it was me.'

—— 21 ——

Daniel felt her drifting from him, in contemplation of this imaginary slight.

'The worst thing is, I'm forgetting it too. Timon's face, the sound of his voice.'

Jane was puzzled. 'You must have photographs?'

'Drawerfuls. My great-aunt's kept the lot. You're right, it's not the face exactly. But the way he walked, the way his expression changed – that's gone. His soul's gone.' Daniel looked hard at his palms, reading the lines on them. 'I was only ten. Sometimes I can't tell the real memories from what got added in later. Does that sound crazy?'

He looked round quickly, to catch her laughing at him. But Jane's expression was solemn. A pursing of the lips had puffed her cheeks out slightly. He loved that slight plumpness. And it did not sound crazy at all, she said.

The bell rang for the first lesson of the afternoon. It was maths, and he and Jane were in different classes.

'Look, if you want to talk about it again,' Jane began.

'Yes?'

'Well, I don't mind listening.'

But Daniel was ashamed, and keen to throw this mood off. The bell had broken it. 'I'm sorry. I didn't mean to dump on you like this.'

Jane sighed, and nodded slightly as she picked up her bag. 'Oh well.' She made her way up the corridor. As she went through the fire doors Daniel remembered to ask: 'But can I see you anyway?'

'When?' Jane shouted.

'Tonight?'

'I'm busy tonight.' The fire doors closed.

'Tomorrow then!'

He thought he saw her raise her hand, before a

stream of children flooded the corridor behind and hid her. That might have been a yes. Or a goodbye, or even an 'I can't hear you.' It might have been 'Get stuffed.' Either way, Daniel couldn't believe his own stupidity. Jane had sat there offering to be his confidante – and he had turned her down! In the agony of it he picked up his bag, turned in the opposite direction towards the maths class – and tried to remember how to find the area between two curves.

Jane dawdled by the river on the way home, hung back with Meg Aitken when she stopped to tread out one cigarette and light a second (tricky that, in the quickening wind) and was generally hard to follow. But she did not see Daniel tracking her. He was extra careful. He felt silly to be doing it at all, though. Shops offered him some shelter, but then it was a long, wide street cross-stitched with houses, where the girls would only have to look back to see him stranded on the pavement. He was forced to dip below cars, hug saplings – things too foolish to think about. If Meg would just leave her alone! He was aching to talk with Jane again. Something like indigestion, something more like fear – that was love as he had found it. It was in the guts, not the heart.

They had arrived at the turning to Meg's street. Jane lived two streets down. They were parting, now. Meg was walking off at last. Now was the moment. Daniel rushed forward and caught Jane's bag.

Jane leapt back. 'Daniel! You gave me a heart attack.'

'Sorry.'

'You don't go leaping out at people like that! Don't you know it's getting dark?'

'I didn't want Meg to see me.'

'No?'

'I wanted to talk to you alone.'

'Meg saw you half a mile back. We both did, prancing about. You'll never make the Secret Service, Daniel.'

Daniel was ashamed. 'I suppose she was laughing at me.'

'She kept up a running commentary in her compact mirror. You idiot! Why didn't you just come and say you wanted to talk?'

'I make things hard for myself,' muttered Daniel, subdued. 'You don't need to tell me that.'

'Not just for yourself,' complained Jane. 'You've given Meg ammunition for a week.'

'I like to see you, what's wrong with that?'

'Nothing, except the way you go about it. Just *talk* to me! I'm not locked in a tower or something: you don't need to kill any dragons.'

Daniel smiled. 'And those fairy-tale girls never laugh in your face.'

'I'm not laughing.'

Jane wasn't laughing, that was true.

'I wish you had more *self-respect*,' she said.

They passed under the railway bridge. A freight train clanked over, taking rock from the quarry to the railhead. They were shoring up the sea-walls, Jane told him, near the new Exhibition Centre. Her father was an engineer: a student of Archimedes should be interested. Beyond the bridge the road split in two, one branch a cul-de-sac with Jane's house at the far end. Daniel was trying to explain how Max, in turn, made money. His company, *Signs of the Times*, was a design consultancy – but what did he actually do?

'This is my gate,' said Jane, putting her hand on the

latch. Her house lay at the end of a short path, gravel between neat ranks of daffodils. Daniel had never been there before, and hoped she would ask him in after all. He had felt her soften towards him, being sensitive to all her sudden moods. She glanced at the kitchen, where light slit the venetian blind. The other rooms were black.

'There's just my mum home. I suppose you could come into the lounge.'

'Thanks.' Daniel noted her caution. 'Don't they like you bringing people in?'

Jane smiled. 'Depends, doesn't it?'

She stroked the St Christopher around her neck.

A man on a mountain bike was approaching them from the far end of the street. As he reached Jane's house he hoisted one foot clear of his crossbar and coasted the last few feet. The light on his bicycle dimmed as he drew up. 'Roaming in the gloaming,' sang Jane's father. His beard wagged at them. 'But it's a night to be in the warm. We haven't met, have we?'

'Daniel is in my tutor group,' said Jane, hastily.

'Under the care of Mr Marx, then?'

'You could say.'

'Jane's always singing his praises. And is science a particular subject of yours, Daniel?'

'I don't think I have any particular subjects.' Daniel glanced uncomfortably at Jane.

Her father smiled faintly. 'I think you'd better be getting in, Jane. Choir practice at six-thirty – don't want you catching something. There's moisture in the air.'

'I forgot,' Jane said apologetically to Daniel. 'I'm meant to be singing tonight: *Belshazzar's Feast*.'

'But not if you don't get there in time. Nice to meet you, Daniel.'

Mr Garfield was wheeling his bike between them, up the garden path. Somehow Jane was caught in its wake and swept away too. 'See you next term!' she called, and squeezed her lips into a smile under the porch light.

'Yes,' said Daniel. At school he would see her. But he would not talk to her alone again, Meg Aitken would make sure of it. He returned to the top of Jane's road, where the pavement curled westward to a sunset that was now blood-red. That was one way home, the long way by foot. He turned and started on the walk to Morton's Holt.

Three

AUNT JENKINS LISTENED OVER THE TELEVISION. That was the sound of Lisa leaving. And that was the sound of Ruby coming in. And Daniel, now. She looked for her watch, and found it on the cushion beside her. It was almost five o'clock. Lisa had said to turn the oven on, for the steak and kidney. But *Newsround* was doing a feature on dolphins. The dolphins were dying, and the pie could wait. Better still—

'Daniel!'

Daniel wandered in. 'Yes?' He looked tired.

'Put the steak and kidney pie in the oven, will you love?' said Aunt Jenkins. Daniel grunted, and retreated towards the kitchen. Aunt Jenkins called after: 'Don't you want to know the right temperature? And what's happened to your face?'

Daniel turned slowly. 'So what temperature should I put it at?'

'Gas Mark 6.'

'That'll be about 200°C, right?'

'If you say so. You know I don't like electric ovens.' Dolphins were dying out there, and all Daniel could do was make difficulties! 'I'll do it myself,' Aunt Jenkins sighed, reaching for her stick.

'Sit down for goodness' sake!'

He slipped the frozen pie into the oven, having basted it with milk. Ruby's bag hung by the door, and over his head orchestral music played. He checked his face in the mirror – one of Gabriel's fists had caught him in the temple.

There was a note from his mother propped against the teapot. Daniel glanced at it, and went upstairs. At the top of the landing the door to Timon's room was open. That was unusual. Max, or perhaps Ruby, had been messing about in there. Probably Max, searching out some beloved disc of his. Although it was still called Timon's room, it had become a store for all their possessions – those that had not yet found a permanent home. Better to use the space than let it become a shrine, Lisa had said. And Lisa, as ever, had been right.

Daniel let his sports bag slide down his arm to the floor. Timon's room could not be called a shrine – not when it contained all Max's jazz records and the clothes horse, and a camp bed for visitors that snapped shut like a pair of jaws if you sat on the hinge. Last autumn he and Ruby had painted the walls in fleshy pink, and Max had bought them dinner for their trouble. That room was no shrine. It held, Daniel felt sure, no ghosts.

But once, when he was younger, he had looked up from the garden and seen Timon's face rippling under the window pane, shrouded by green curtains. At the top of the landing he had heard the ping of a spit pellet as it smacked into the bin, and seen the faint light seep from beneath the door. He had run to his own room and locked it, because Timon was nearby. But that was in the past. He no longer thought himself haunted. Timon's place was nowhere in the world.

'Penny for them?' Ruby had slipped in behind him.

Daniel looked up wryly. 'Haven't you heard of inflation?'

'Second-hand thoughts ought to come cheaper. And yours aren't new, I'll bet.'

'They're a bit soiled,' Daniel said. 'You're welcome to them.'

But she didn't ask again. 'Have you seen Lisa?'

'She left a note.'

Lisa would not be back for a while. 'Get your own tea again,' was what the note had amounted to, though it covered two sides of paper. Lisa always wrote more when she felt guilty.

'She's been very secretive recently.' Ruby sounded suspicious to match. 'Assignations, mysterious absences. It's odd.'

'Yeah, you'd think she had a life of her own,' said Daniel.

'You would, little step-brother, you would.' Ruby added slyly: 'Perhaps more than one.'

'What do you mean?'

'Oh nothing,' she said in a voice which meant the opposite. Daniel picked up his bag and went down the landing to his room. Sketched faces lined each wall, in pastel or ink – he had a talent for such things. He took a textbook out and pressed it open at the right page for his homework. Looking up, he found that Ruby had followed him. She was dark-skinned, like Max. Her dark hair curled down in front of her dark eyes. Daniel didn't like her talking that way about his mother.

'Is there something you're trying to tell me?'

'No, it's too bizarre. I'm probably wrong.'

'Let's say I'll forgive you.'

'If only it were that simple!'

She came in and sat on the bed, hands clasped in

front of her. 'Try sleeping next door to the bathroom some time. There've been some pretty gross scenes in there recently. Mornings in particular.'

'You think Mum's ill?'

'Mad perhaps, not ill. Oh dear! Do I have to spell it out?'

'If you're trying to tell me she's pregnant you needn't bother. I already know.'

'You *know*?' Ruby's astonishment had barely registered before it was drowned in a flash flood of indignation. 'You mean they told you? But I'm two years older!'

'Calm down, no one's said anything. Mum got one of those test kits. I saw the packet when I took the rubbish out. Didn't need a genius to guess something was going on.' Daniel ruled a neat line under the title of his essay. Then he shut the book and slipped it away for later. 'Besides, she's been hanging over the baby pictures in catalogues. I've seen it coming.'

Ruby managed to damp down her rage, but was not satisfied. 'So what do you think about it?' she demanded grudgingly.

Daniel shrugged. 'It's their business, I suppose.'

'It's not their business. Nappies, feeds, walks – we'll be getting the brunt of it. Oh, and ugh!'

'What is it?'

'I was just thinking – what they must have done. All those rolls of fat!'

'How d'you think *you* got here?' Daniel laughed.

'That was a long time ago,' sniffed Ruby. 'I wasn't around to hear it.'

Daniel looked at her in amusement. Ruby was making fun of herself with that sniff; but the distaste was real too. She was a strange mixture, which he couldn't resist stirring. 'It's just nature,' he said stolidly.

'Nature's best left on the Serengeti ...' She paused. 'Oh, don't tell me you're pleased.'

'I'm happy for them,' Daniel intoned in a flat voice. 'It will be nice to have a little brother or sister.'

'Oh *God*!' Ruby stalked from the room.

Daniel leaned back in his chair. He didn't mean to annoy Ruby, but somehow couldn't stop himself. The way she put her feelings on display – they festooned her like bunting. It was safer to seem to despise it. While he – how had he got like this? – was secretive, ungenerous. He had become a person he did not like.

Sometimes he tried to trace that thread to its beginning. Timon had something to do with it, no doubt; but the start was even earlier, when his father had left. Val used to get drunk, but smashing-things drunk, not showing-off drunk like Max. Val had gone north with another woman, and they'd never seen him again. She had children of her own, and didn't fancy taking his on board, that was the story. Well, said Timon, he let himself agree to that. He didn't have to.

Six months later Timon was dead. It didn't matter what the postmortem said. Lisa knew Val was responsible. Though he was three hundred miles away, sitting in a semi-detached with a can of beer in his hand, Val might as well have held a gun to his son's head. If it hadn't been for Val, Timon wouldn't have made the friends he did, he wouldn't have needed to escape, or taken such a desperate path. Timon was too much like Val in every way.

And yes, it was a hard situation for Ruby to find herself in. Before, she had lived alone with her father in a flat on the harbour front. It was new and expensive, but Max had been too sentimental to sell when Ruby's mother died. At thirteen Ruby had become cook and housekeeper. She had taught herself to do Max's accounts on her mother's old PC. Spreadsheets, debit and credit: she took it off his hands. Max was proud of her. He knew there were not many daughters like Ruby.

Then suddenly, the flat he had not had the heart to sell was sold after all. He was marrying Lisa, and they were moving into Morton's Holt. Ruby became a teenager once again, overnight – because her father wanted it that way.

Daniel contemplated his jigsaw life. How would the pieces arrange themselves this time? With himself nearer the edge, and a little smaller, spinning out of the main picture. And Ruby, spinning out too. And Timon gone altogether, to make room. The room which would soon have its old nursery paper back. He put his textbook away, and started sketching out a new face on his drawing-pad, a baby's sleeping face in dark pastels.

Outside, Max had just got out of his car. He paused for a minute, looking up at the house. It was a mess – the puzzle of gable ends, the Gothic decoration turretting the roof. He wondered how someone like Lisa could have consented to live in such a raddled, *ugly* place, sick aunt or no. And why she would not hear of leaving even now. Was it nostalgia for her first husband, the Irishman, who had loved it? The thought provoked a dull jealousy. But Max was not a man to nurse it. As he shifted from foot to foot his mood shifted too. The house had its charms. Forget the heating bill, forget the rising damp: the view from their bedroom on a spring morning could almost persuade him that he was indeed a knee-britched squire – a fancy he had gradually come (without quite realising it) to cherish. Hills, woods, pasture – and in the distance an urban smudge where other, less fortunate people lived. Without the smudge it would not have been so satisfying. He needed those other people, to taste their drabness, and then to drink in the nectar of self-contemplation. He, Max Hilliard, was not of their stamp.

Max finished his cigarette and threw it in the water butt. From the dining-room window he had just seen Aunt Jenkins' moon face, waxily regarding him. Nosy woman. Her gaping mouth, so like a trout's, reminded him of a shock he'd had that morning as he searched for a clean pair of socks. A practical joke, if you could call it that – and Daniel was the culprit. Gratefully he turned to a matter on which he could act. Things to do, there. It was not an isolated incident: would that it were. Lisa might blind herself to Daniel's … *oddnesses*, but that did him no favours in the end, Max said to himself. It was time they had a serious talk.

Meanwhile Daniel's baby had proved unsatisfactory, and he had smothered its blunt face in pastel blankets.

'Ah Daniel, I was hoping I might find you alone.'

Max's head appeared at the door.

'I often am alone,' said Daniel.

'But not so easy to find,' Max smiled, and taking this as an invitation came in. He turned the wooden chair opposite Daniel's desk and sat astride it, wearing the man-to-man look that men use when they speak to boys. Glancing at the drawing above Daniel's bed he nodded approval. 'You know how to catch a likeness.'

'Thanks.'

'Anyone I've met?'

'It's my attempt at … the soul of something.'

'Ah, the soul ...' Max looked understanding. Other paintings and drawings stared at them from the walls. All showed faces, human or animal. The largest was a broad leafy face, peering from a bush. Or perhaps the face *was* the bush. Twigs ran like veins, like furrows in the skin that was only leaves, green and shadowed by a light from beneath, within. The eyes were owl's eyes.

'I have you to thank for the present in my sock drawer this morning, I think.'

Daniel looked up, surprised. He had forgotten, for the moment, what he had done with his catch. 'You mean the carp?'

'Of course the carp.'

'I'm sorry, it was childish to leave it there.'

'So why do it?' asked Max with asperity.

Daniel's eyes flicked towards the window as if he might find his morning self outside and ask him. 'I was annoyed, I suppose. I'll wash your socks for you.'

'That's hardly the point. What possessed you in the first place? What had I done to deserve that?'

Max's voice ascended a tone in asking this question, to which the answer was so obviously 'Nothing at all' that Daniel could not bring himself to say it.

'Put it down to hormones. Or bad blood.' Daniel's veins felt treacly and sluggish. Bad blood might be the answer.

Max was talking to the leafy face. 'Perhaps I've let you have your head too much.'

'Don't worry about my head, Max. It's not your concern.'

'It is if it upsets your mother. She tries so hard to make your life happy, Daniel. We both do. And sometimes we feel it's just being thrown back at us.'

Ruby appeared in the doorway behind her father and

pulled her yak face: solemn, ruminant. Daniel smiled. Max had just that way of chewing at his lip. Max looked behind him, but too late to catch her.

'I don't know what to tell you,' said Daniel.

'And now it looks as if you're getting into fights. It's all so wearing.'

A choking yell from downstairs brought them both out onto the landing. There was a sharp crash, and a whimper in which they recognised the voice of Aunt Jenkins. Max was first to the ground floor. Through the open door they could see Aunt Jenkins, standing alone in the conservatory. A paperweight – a blue marble nymph – lay broken on the tiled floor. Above it the wooden sill had been dented by the force of its impact. Aunt Jenkins was returning to the wicker throne from which she had evidently just staggered.

'It was *him*!' she cried. 'It *was* him! Wasn't it?'

'You've been having nightmares,' said Max a little brusquely, putting his arm round her shoulder. Concern for his wife's aunt was already tempered by grief for the broken nymph.

'His face up against the glass like that, ready to frighten me out of my wits. Such a thoughtless young man. But I showed him! He soon made off when he saw that stone girl flying.' Aunt Jenkins chuckled cunningly.

'Who do you mean?' asked Ruby, who had followed them down.

'Timon, of course! I always said he was irresponsible, but this!' She flopped into the scatter cushions. 'What are we going to do?'

'Get a dustpan, Ruby love,' said Max.

As Ruby left, they heard the front door shut two rooms away.

'Here's Lisa,' said Max, relieved to hear his wife returning early. 'She'll know how to handle it.'

Lisa did know. Quickly the floor was swept and the nymph consigned (without regret on Lisa's part) to the bin. And Aunt Jenkins was allowed to tell her story: how she had nodded off, and woken to see Timon's face pressed against the conservatory glass. How she'd seen it on other recent occasions. How she'd opened the door that very morning to Timon's insistent knock. It was all quite terrible. Lisa and Max exchanged significant glances over her head. But Lisa knew the right things to say. By degrees Aunt Jenkins was brought to talk of other things, of memories less painful – of Tolly. Soon she was comfortably settled in the living-room, with the television on and a pile of photo albums at her side.

Four

THE ALBUMS WERE HER PRIZED POSSESSIONS, A lovely nest for her memories, her little chicks. Aunt Jenkins loved to visit the stationers, to squish the grandest covers and feel them yield to her finger, to trace their gilt finery with her nail. Home she would come with a roll of cellophane or a sachet of corner-fixers. The family history was laid flat between her pages.

It had begun when she was a young woman, newly-married. With Tolly away in the war, photographs had meant so much. There he stood in front of a tank with all his friends, somewhere in the northern desert. Or at their wedding, already in uniform, with his best man Freddy who was killed. Aunt Jenkins turned several pages to find Lisa's wedding, and herself grinning in a hat with a white flying-saucer brim. She frowned. Lisa's young man – of course he had not turned out well, yet he had a charm with him, the way the Irish do. He could do tricks, produce an egg from someone's ear. He had clever fingers.

Daniel watched his great-aunt humming, a slice of Madeira beside her. On television the children's presenter was getting worked up about the next programme – or was it the last? A green felt alien was giving him a hard time. Aunt Jenkins was not watching, but Daniel knew it was silence she could not stand. At last she noticed him near her.

'Daniel!'

'What are you looking at?'

'You, my dear.'

Daniel peered, and saw her finger lying across a playground photo, where on a roundabout his own infant figure was spread-eagled. In the picture Timon was pushing him round, as he had often done – faster and faster, before tearing away at a tangent while Daniel was left to grip the rail in terror. Timon had fooled him that way every time. He felt it now, and the shame at having believed his brother yet again: 'I'll give you a gentle push this time, Daniel, just a little one.' Sick with giddiness Daniel had made a jump for it, and cut his elbow on the concrete. His father, when he saw the tear in his shirt, had added a bruise for luck. And Lisa had said nothing.

'That's not me,' Daniel said. 'I was just a kid then.'

'You'll always be a child to me, Daniel.'

'Things change.'

But clearly Aunt Jenkins was not satisfied. The last bit of Madeira was sliding round the plate.

'Just a little push, Daniel. Just hold on tight.' Timon always fooled him that way.

Aunt Jenkins flipped the pages of the album with her left thumb. A look of pleasure lit her as she found an earlier incarnation. 'I had a face then, as faces go,' she sighed.

'You still have a very distinguished one, let me tell you.' It was Lisa who declared this, as she backed into the living-room with a tray and a fresh pot of tea. She was spoiling her aunt today, for beside the pot was a second slice of cake, set off with a spray of cherry blossom. 'There are plenty younger who'd swap.'

'There are plenty of young fools,' commented Aunt Jenkins.

Lisa folded down the legs of the tray and placed it on the chair, over Aunt Jenkins' knees. 'Do you like the blossom? There was so much on the lawn, it would be a shame to let it go to waste.'

Aunt Jenkins glanced at it. 'We haven't had a proper spring at all this year.'

Lisa took this as an attempt at conversation. 'The storms did a lot of damage. The road to Mereton was still flooded yesterday.'

Aunt Jenkins nodded. 'There are children born with webbed feet at Mereton, that's what they used to say. Gills, occasionally.'

'And it's cold, too. Come into the kitchen with me – you'll find it cosy there with the oven. There's something I need to talk to you about.'

'Oh, I'm warm enough in myself. Is this *Mars Ranch 3000*?' The alien had donned a stetson, and a rattle of drums brought Aunt Jenkins' favourite programme on to the screen.

Lisa admitted defeat. She took the tray away.

Daniel followed her into the kitchen. 'That blasted television!' she fumed. She cut a slice of Madeira for herself and ate it in two exasperated gulps.

'What was it you wanted to talk about?'

'Oh, nothing,' said Lisa briskly. 'I just want to get her out of herself. She sits in that chair too much.'

'Let her watch if she wants to. There's no harm.'

'I hate to see her dwindling away, that's all. You probably don't remember what she used to be like. I've never known anyone with so much energy.'

Daniel did remember, just. A different Aunt Jenkins, haughty and generous, lived on in a few memories from his infancy. But the years between, like a thick lacquer, had overlaid those memories and changed them.

Lisa herself had changed no less. The woman who had been too scared to stand up to his father was no one's pushover now. Lisa's losses might have crushed her, but in adversity she had become strong. She had fought, with the council and the bank and everybody. Though Aunt Jenkins had mortgaged the house to prop up one of Val's schemes, somehow Lisa had saved it. Without qualifications she had gone to college, re-inventing herself as a legal secretary. She had kept Daniel in food and clothes, and while Aunt Jenkins began her long drift into senility had seen to it that she stayed comfortable. Lisa's hair had greyed a little, but a bottle of henna hid that.

Yet Daniel thought her older when he found her late that evening. Lisa was in the conservatory, singing: a sad song and a slow one, picked out with delicate fingers from the hollow of an old guitar.

> *You told me that you needed me,*
> *You told me it was life or death.*
> *I never believed a word, my love:*
> *You were wasting your shallow breath ...*

Daniel knew the song. He had heard his mother sing it on the old CD. Her voice was deeper now – something about it was deeper. It wobbled on the last note, that narrow promontory into the waiting silence. She left off, but still the fingers played, rowed her forward through the silence, and landed her safely.

Daniel came in. 'That was beautiful.'

His mother sat cross-legged on the floor, amidst the ferns and cheese plants. 'Daniel! I thought you'd gone out.'

'People always think I'm out.'

'You do glide about very quietly, my little barn owl.'

'You haven't sung that for years,' he said.

'It came into my head when I saw the guitar. I don't know who left it out here in the sun. It was a mile out of tune.'

'That was me, sorry. I found it in Timon's room a couple of days ago. Behind Max's portfolio.'

'You were teaching yourself?'

'That I'm tone deaf, at least. Mum, why don't you play any more?'

'Tone deaf!'

'But why don't you play? You never even put on the CDs now.'

Lisa had been nearly famous once, lead singer of a band. Daniel's earliest memories were of the crowded sunshine at a festival somewhere, the roar that went up with the first few bars of a favourite song, the sweat and rush backstage, and how the tattooed roadies made a fuss of him. Lisa had worn a long patchwork skirt that swung from her hips. Val had watched her from the wings.

'Some doors are better kept shut,' said Lisa.

'You shouldn't have to give up all the good memories. It isn't fair.'

'Memories!' she repeated contemptuously, but got up smiling.

'You were big. Remember Knebworth.'

'And Yeovil Church Hall. We only took off in the last year. Before that … Oh well, it's all invisible.'

'You could do it again. You can get another manager, a proper one.'

Lisa laughed, and took his hand. 'Sometimes you talk like a child. I haven't the energy, believe me. There are all kinds of reasons.'

'Give me six.'

She paused. 'I gather from Max that you already know the chief one.'

'What do you mean?' Daniel began cautiously.

'Ruby had a confrontation with him earlier. It's true, I'm going to have a baby.'

'I see.'

'I'm sorry we didn't tell you before, love. It's not that we didn't want to, but the right moment is usually long gone by the time you recognise it.'

'It's true, then?' Daniel repeated.

Smiling, Lisa nodded. Her eyes were moist.

The hairs on Daniel's arm prickled. Though he'd known to expect this, he stared as if he had been taken quite by surprise. He had not known, in fact, how it would feel to hear those words out loud.

'Congratulations, Mum,' he said at last. He came and kissed her, stooped with a middle-aged peck to the cheek. There couldn't have been a chaster, more fraudulent kiss. 'I'm pleased for you.'

'And for yourself, I hope, darling.'

'And for myself, of course,' he said.

Something had woken Ruby. Although she had heard nothing there had been a noise, for certain. The house was silent, and the countryside beyond –

silent in the stealthy way her town-bred mind mistrusted. But the echo of a noise still buzzed about her. A child crying ... She sat up, and reached for the switch of her bedside lamp, but did not press it. Was there an intruder in the house? The thought sent the blood rushing away from her brain, and left her cold and fearful. Then she heard Max turn over in bed in the next room, and the bedsprings creak. That helped a little. Also she remembered something of her dream, enough to make her think the sound a fantasy. A stupid nightmare – about a baby of all things! She put her hand to her face, and flinched.

Unsteadily she manoeuvred her feet to the ground, and stood before the full-length mirror on the wardrobe door. Her moonlit reflection was intact, and just as she had left it: from the oval face with its stark black fringe, down through an epidemic of measled pyjamas to her bare feet, curling into the rug. That was her, the whole of her, framed in the mirror. It seemed all at once a very small thing, to be Ruby Hilliard – when everything else in the world was not. She wished her father would roll over again, and make the bedsprings groan.

So the baby was now official – and another family secret punctured. Ruby had come back to Morton's Holt with a secret of her own to nurse, a secret principally from Lisa. She'd been planning to spring it when the time seemed right – when Lisa's smile was broadest. But she found now that she had lost the taste for such things.

A wand of light lay on the floor, thrown down by the moon. Ruby had never noticed moonlight in the city. Before she moved here she had never seen the Milky Way, never heard an owl. She stepped to the curtain and drew it back a little. The room faced away from the road, towards the woods and the canal. Half an acre of rough grass lay between them and the ornamental foliage of the garden. Each tree stood in its own pool of silver, and the lawn wore a wreath of dark leaves. One object near the house puzzled her at first. Its shadow was a pair of long antennae peering from a turtle's shell. But of course – it was an upturned wheelbarrow. Ruby smiled at its strangeness, the strangeness of a world corrupted by the moon's silver. There was the laurel hedge, looking more than ever like a sleeping dragon; and the magnolia tree that had pierced its side. Nearby, a small sapling seemed to be waving to her, arm upraised.

She glanced away, about to let the curtain fall, when something drew her back. The sapling's trunk had swollen to twice its width. And now it had split, and become something else – something that in any other place would have been quite unremarkable. A pair of human legs. A young man stood in the garden below. He was as thin as a sapling after all, and in this light his braided hair might be taken easily for catkins or hanging blossom. He was waving. Though she could not see his face, Ruby had no doubt that he was smiling up at her, too. Yes, he knew all about the fear that had seized her by the throat. He was enjoying the effect. Ruby could not scream; she could barely breathe. Abruptly the young man turned and began to walk back towards the wood. His pace was lazy, yet he covered the ground quickly in long, rolling strides: before Ruby could persuade her legs to step back from the window he was half way across the rough land. Soon he disappeared into the wood.

Next door the bedsprings creaked again, but it was too late. Sleep had forsaken her. Leaving the curtains open she crawled timidly back into her bed, and watched the cold stars slanting through her window.

Five

*I*T WAS SATURDAY AFTERNOON, AND DANIEL HAD just left Marley's Tearooms. There he earned fifteen pounds each week, washing up and folding napkins, or cutting apple pie into slices. He astonished himself by enjoying the work, and the Irish airs that twanged continually from a speaker overhead. Marley's was a traditional establishment, in a city where most of the food was fast. In other cafés the customers inched plastic trays to the nearest cash till and squirted tea into their cup from a machine. At Marley's the waitresses wore aprons, and Mrs Kinsale saw to it that their caps were starched and ironed, each crease crisp as an apple.

At quarter to six he was in the city centre, and thinking about a bus. Being late he decided to come back through the pedestrian precinct. It was not a good place to be as darkness fell. The wind, slinking through, spent itself against the concrete and the metal shutters. The few people still about quickened their pace: sales and empty shop lights could not slow them. Nearby, gulls teemed out over the water that Daniel could neither hear nor see. But its smell was everywhere.

Suddenly it had become night; and, as if at a signal, the empty precinct began to fill again. Near the pentagon of benches at its centre a group of youths appeared. Another group spilt from the subway steps, and slalomed down a row of bay trees. The trees were made giddy in their tubs as they circled, hanging to the trunks. They glowed with a dark energy, fuelled by boredom: soon they would need a new amusement. Quickly Daniel turned into an alley matted with paper bags and glass. A cat was pawing at the contents of a shopping trolley, which moved slightly as it leapt away. There was a shout from behind. A glance reassured him – the revellers were arguing over a bottle, as one teetered along the top of a bench. But his throat was dry. He saw a white railing at the far end of the alley, then the harbour. He stumbled, then ran between the narrow walls towards it.

He reached the railing and gulped at the air, as the wind slapped his cheeks. His stomach was moving: his body seemed to think it was at sea. It was a slight dizziness, which lessened as he gripped the rail. He knew where he was now. Nearby stood a fountain, with sea gods and mermaids: Triton, Tethys, Lir. Their crowns were green with oxide, spears soot-tipped. From this quay, in the old days, ships had sailed with slaves, and brought tobacco home. The bolts for the manacles were still in the wall. It had been Black Boy Quay.

Daniel moved along the rail, towards a quayside warehouse now made over to restaurants and bars and a shopping arcade. It would be easy to catch a bus from there. Or – he checked his pocket – he might sit out a couple of hours in the nearby arts cinema, watching subtitles. Not to understand would be a treat. It occurred to him that his family might soon begin to wonder where he was. A childish pleasure hovered round the thought. In his imagination his description was being circulated to the squad cars, while an inspector drank tea in the living-room, knees tucked nervously together. 'You'll probably find he's visiting a girl-friend. After all, he's a growing lad.' But of course no one would have noticed he was gone, yet. Ruby was out, Lisa and Max were celebrating at the other end of town. As for Aunt Jenkins – her mind was off the hook, and no one could get through. Four pound coins clunked in his palm.

'Got any spare change?'

A boy in a Balaclava was sitting at his feet. His legs were wrapped in a dirty blanket. Swollen fingers cupped a dish, in which some coins already lay, as an encouragement. The boy's eyes met Daniel's, then moved away. Daniel let a guilty coin drop into the dish.

'Daniel March always had a generous nature. It will be his undoing.'

Two more figures were huddled a little further down the arcade, near the cinema entrance. One of them had spoken. Daniel walked forward cautiously.

'Do I know you?' he asked.

The nearest was a girl. The other one, the speaker, was contemplating the pattern of the stitching on his rucksack. 'You should know me,' he said, and looked up. 'You should know me.'

Daniel felt his legs giving way, and the dizziness of a few seconds before crash upon him like a wave. He knew that this could not be happening. This was some freak vision. He would wake up soon.

'Timon? Is it you?'

Timon leaned forward sharply and hissed: 'Be careful what you say.'

It was Timon's voice. The face was thin. Timon's round chin was speckled with bristle. His hair was braided roughly; teeth yellow. But what a smile! Timon's smile, that once could light a room up, electric! And now with yellow teeth.

'*Big Issue?*' said the girl beside him. She had a pile of magazines to sell. Recklessly Daniel gave her some more money, Timon watching him. On his hands was written in red ink, 'H-O-M-E-L-E-S-S.' A letter for each finger.

'Like a dog, me.' said Timon. 'Looking for a good owner.'

The girl sniggered.

'But remember, I'm not just for Christmas. I'm for life.'

'It's spring, you idiot!' sniggered the girl.

'I'm not wrong?' said Daniel. 'It is you?'

'Touch me if you like.' Timon offered his hand for touching, and Daniel flinched from it. 'On second thoughts, save it till I've had a wash. Don't want you catching my germs.'

Daniel looked – there were *things* crawling on Timon's blanket.

'Where have you been?' he asked.

Timon yawned, and a smell of dampness shrouded them, a chill that made Daniel want to hug himself. 'I can't remember all the places.' He shook his blanket, and the things became tiny black flies and flew off down the arcade. One settled on Daniel's hand; he wiped it away, a smear of blood among the wings and the delicate body casing.

'Were you waiting here for me?' he asked.

A smart couple veered to the far side of the pavement at the sight of them. The girl beside Timon offered them a *Big Issue*, but they did not glance at her as they headed to a nearby restaurant, to be wrapped in the soft folds of the money world.

'I wasn't waiting,' Timon said vaguely. 'People come and go. They come, sometimes, and mostly they go. No one stays long.'

'I haven't gone,' said Daniel.

'I know. I'm glad you haven't. You might have taken one look and run.' But this made Timon serious. 'Perhaps you ought to run. I'm bad news, little brother. Go home.' His eyes moved beyond Daniel, to the place in the harbour where the city lights danced like submerged flame.

'Home? And leave you? When I've not seen you in six years?'

Timon nodded a little. 'If you like, buy me a cup of tea.'

Timon left his blanket with the magazine girl. Also a bag of clothes no one seemed likely to steal. Another smaller bag he took with him. It was an elaborate procedure for one who had nothing, and he moved with a languid slowness. When he stumbled at a paving stone Daniel realised why – he was on the point of exhaustion.

'You don't sleep well here,' Timon said. 'You sleep with one eye open. People take your things. Beat you. The police aren't too interested.' He could hardly talk for weariness.

Roy's was nearest: a greasy spoon café where Timon would not look too out of place. Daniel bought them tea in mugs, and a bacon butty for Timon whose hands were so cold. Behind the counter shone chrome kettles and urns. Roy's moustache twitched a little.

'Is he with you?'

Timon was breathing on the window, writing his

name and drawing pictures in the mist. One or two people had stopped outside the café to watch as he began to press his nose against the glass. 'Tell him to knock it off, will you? I've a living to make.'

'I'll tell him. Sorry.'

'I'd appreciate it.' Roy dolloped chips and beans on to the plate. 'Have a nice meal. This is on me. And don't bring him back, eh?'

'I guess I've got some explaining to do,' said Timon as he took the plate. He shook salt onto the chips, more than was reasonable, till they glittered like quartz. 'Want some?'

Daniel shook his head. He could look at him properly now – in the arcade the light had been bad. He *looked* like Timon. The eyes and mouth were his. But six years on, everything else had changed, the whole face thinned. The hair was lighter, with the stain of some dye just growing out near the tips. Timon's hands were thinner too, and shook a little as he held the mug. *Homeless* was not just written in biro – Daniel saw it was a tattoo.

He needed to be sure.

'You remember that time we camped out on Exmoor? You look like you've only just got back.'

'I remember,' smiled Timon. 'Dad had to dig a latrine.'

'And the stove wouldn't light. And the caravan almost rolled into a stream.' Daniel's laughter could not hide the fact that he was probing.

'It was a tent, Daniel. Almost blew away. Is your memory playing tricks?'

Timon looked at him impassively. He knew Daniel didn't trust him, perhaps. But then he could hardly expect it. 'Yes, it was a tent, I guess,' said Daniel.

'That's settled then. Unless you want to see the birthmark on my behind.'

'Not necessary,' Daniel said, ashamed.

'Good, because this place isn't much warmer than the arcade.' Timon dabbled a chip in the sauce from the beans. 'Now we've settled who I am, you can ask me questions.'

'If you want me to,' said Daniel, who was not sure what to ask. He wanted to prolong the moment – him and Timon together again, at last. Knowledge would probably spoil it.

On the window Timon had drawn a heart, and the condensation had made it bleed. That was a place to begin. 'The girl who was with you. Are you together?'

Timon smiled, and Daniel saw the question had fallen wide. 'She's living dangerously, on the run from Daddy and a gang of private tutors. Six months from now she'll be home with a story to tell, and a superior expression. She'll have had her wild time.' Timon produced a cigarette from his little bag, and, to Daniel's surprise, an expensive-looking lighter. 'Of course, she may not be so lucky.'

'What do you mean?'

'A lot of things can happen.'

'You mean, on the street?'

Blue smoke jetted from Timon's pursed mouth. 'I mean anywhere.'

Daniel followed his gaze to a TV on the wall of the café, where an office block was blazing in the night. A hundred lives wrecked by one bomb, somewhere. 'But on the street ...'

'It's true, there are dangers,' said Timon.

'You don't say much for someone with a lot of explaining to do,' Daniel observed drily.

'It's one of the habits I've got out of. Give me time. Soon I'll be blossoming. Singing like a canary.' Timon grinned, and Daniel found his eye drawn to the gaps where his top and bottom teeth should be. Gaps, one up two down. That'll be where the seabed knocked his mouth, thought Daniel, but the thought had no business there. If Timon was not a ghost.

'You can start by telling me how you happen not to be dead.'

Timon looked coy. 'It was a set-up. They wanted me to disappear for a while, become a non-person. I had to oblige.'

'"They"?'

'We won't go into names. Let's just say these are not people you refuse to co-operate with. When they tell you to get on your bike, you don't stop pedalling till the chain breaks.'

'These ... people. What did they have against you?' persisted Daniel. Timon's explanation seemed too conveniently anonymous.

'Oh, a misunderstanding,' said Timon dismissively, 'a question of a hundred pounds here or there. They made me an offer – to get out while I still had my skin. I wasn't about to say no.'

This didn't make sense to Daniel. 'But they found your body.'

'*A* body. Not mine. The fish had been at it by then. I don't know whose it was – some kid who had it coming. They needed a body, see, to make it look right.'

'But the police identified you.' Daniel tried to remember what it was Max had said. 'The dental records.'

'Science is wonderful. Put someone in a white coat and people will believe anything. Have you ever

—— 53 ——

wondered how much they pay the people in those forensic labs?'

Daniel shrugged.

'Not enough. These people had a lot of money, and every kind of clout. They got the result they wanted.'

Was that possible? Daniel didn't know. Timon's very presence made him feel naïve, just ten again.

'There are tests, though – scientific ones.'

'No one was looking for anything or anyone but me. You don't double-check when you see what you're expecting.'

Timon smiled in a weary way, as if these were facts that ought not to need pointing out.

'I'm sorry,' said Daniel. 'It's so hard to believe. It's like a dream.'

'Yes, I've been living in a dream. But I've come back now. It's not true what I told you. I *was* waiting for you in the arcade – I hoped you'd come. You used to go there sometimes, in the old days.'

'You could have called me at the house. Or outside school – you could have met me coming out one day.'

'And if I had? And you'd told me where to go? I couldn't have stood that, Daniel. You might have, and I wouldn't have blamed you. At least if you walked by me in the arcade I could always pretend to myself that you hadn't recognised me. I've changed so much.'

'Everything's changed.'

'Yes. Everything except you, Daniel.'

'Me too.' Daniel looked down at the tiles, where they lay patterned about his feet. And why shouldn't I have, he thought resentfully. 'After what you did.'

'I see. Well, what has it been like?' asked Timon.

'Like a lot of things. Mum's remarried.'

Timon thumped the table, triumphant. 'I *knew* it! I knew she wouldn't last five minutes without Valentine.'

'You're wrong,' Daniel replied. 'There's more to her than you ever saw.' He remembered how he had watched open-mouthed as Lisa reduced a stiff-lipped council official to blubbering apology. A million miles from the Lisa in Timon's head. You'd never have thought she had it in her.

'And Aunt Jenkins?' asked Timon.

'Losing it. A bit more every day. First it's forgetting which channel the snooker's on, the next week she leaves her library books in the fridge. I suppose it's a textbook case.'

Despite that, Daniel realised, it was the first time he had ever talked about Aunt Jenkins.

Aunt Jenkins had once been sharper than any of them: a dealer in antiquities. Morton's Holt had been earned by her and Tolly's labour. But she was old, and more than old. It was disease that had crippled her mind, and Timon's loss was part of what had made her cease to fight it. After Timon it was easier to forget. Once Daniel had heard her talking to Lisa: 'If you find me wandering,' she said, 'don't hesitate. Just put me in a home. Be kind to yourself, and remember what I went through with Tolly. Think of Tolly.' These days Aunt Jenkins thought of little else. Tolly was her idol, restored by loss to his golden days of track and field. But Lisa would not act. Something stopped her dead. Aunt Jenkins was little trouble after all. On some days she could seem almost herself, though her slips showed it was a facade, brittle as ice, and melting.

'Is this one dead?' Roy was standing beside him, nodding towards Timon's mug. He had a tray of mugs. Daniel shook himself awake, with a feeling that he had been elsewhere. He saw the mug half-empty on the table. Timon had gone.

'My friend – did you see where he went?'

Roy's eyebrows twitched sceptically. 'He left five minutes ago.'

Daniel leapt to his feet. 'But he was here just now!'

'He went five minutes ago, I told you. Good riddance, I should say.'

'That's not true!'

The colour came into Roy's face. 'I don't need this. You go now, OK? This is a clean, quiet place.' The mugs on the tray chinked as Roy's hands shook. 'Look! See what your ... your *friend* has done for my trade!' Daniel looked. The café's tables were deserted. 'I knew he was trouble as soon as he walked in. You think I haven't seen his kind before?'

'Poor people you mean?' retorted Daniel.

'I don't mean *poor*.' Roy spat the word back. 'You are a fool!' He turned away and through the swing doors to the kitchen, where the steam hid him and then the light, and the flaps swinging back, and left Daniel alone.

Six

'D ANIEL? ARE YOU ALL RIGHT?'
Daniel's head was pounding. All the way home, from what he remembered, shocks had sparked from his fingers: he had lit up the dark streets. And now he was in bed, a dreadful lethargy on him. 'Ruby?'

'It's the third time I've called you.'

'I was asleep. I think.'

'If that's sleep, give me insomnia.' Ruby came and opened the window a little. Air steamed from Daniel, raw and sulphurous. The night breeze licked at him through the window, and pimpled his skin. Sitting up, he found he was still dressed.

'Has anyone missed me?'

'Did you want them to, poor thing?' Ruby laughed thinly. 'Sorry, Max and Lisa are having their celebration meal, remember? And as for your Aunt Jenkins—'

'Hang on, Ruby. What time is it?'

'Just past midnight.'

'Ruby!' cried Daniel, clutching his forehead. 'Why did you wake me?' He felt as if he might have slept for days.

'I was worried. When you came in you pushed past me like a zombie. I know you're the surly type, but I thought something must have happened. And the sounds you've been making ...'

'Sounds?'

'I've never heard anything like it. A kind of *gurgling*, but there were words mixed in too. It was awful.'

Daniel groped for the light switch. Ruby was standing at the end of the bed, in her dressing-gown. The worry on her face was real. But there was something else there, in the tautness of her voice, and the way her hands twisted and untwisted the looped bow in her belt.

'What was I saying?'

'I didn't understand any of it. It was like another language. Daniel, where did you go tonight?'

'Out,' said Daniel flatly, trying to remember. After seeing Timon he had wandered, anywhere. He had lost himself several times. Pavements and streets had reared up confusedly, bent back on themselves, and somehow dropped him before his own door at last. 'Just out.'

'That doesn't tell me much.'

'Tough!' he rasped. 'What is it with you? When did you get to be my mother?'

Ruby grimaced. 'I'm trying to help you. Something's happened – I'm right, aren't I?'

A sudden breeze rattled the window. It snatched Daniel away to the colonnades, the ditches, to the creatures that huddled and sought shelter. He felt his fingers grow numb, the dampness seep through him. The walls had grown unaccountably thin – thin as paper. It would take only the smallest push, the slightest warping of the world's frame, for him to join them. But Ruby was talking to him still, and peering at his face.

'You're shivering.'

'I'm fine.'

'Please don't lie to me,' she said. Then she added

quietly, 'You see, I … I think we have to be friends now.'

Daniel looked at her in uncertainty. Ruby was frightened of something, all her precious self-possession frayed to rags.

'I've done nothing, all right? I went for a walk. I went to see a film.'

'OK, what was the title?'

'I don't remember. It was in Polish.'

'I can easily check in the paper, you know. There's really no point in all this.'

'Do what you like,' said Daniel. 'I don't have to explain myself to you.'

Ruby's patience ran out abruptly. Pulling the bow on her dressing-gown tight with a short tug she said, 'Well, if you want to sulk that's your privilege. I thought we could help each other.'

As she turned to leave, she scooped a sock from the floor with her foot. She flicked it into the corner, where Daniel's discarded clothes lay in a heap. 'This place is a tip,' she observed.

He waited till he heard the door close. A few seconds later music, loud and operatic, throbbed through the air. For all his tiredness, Daniel had never felt so aware. Every sense crackled. Moods flooded his mind and shrank back in little multicoloured tides, each with its own salt tang. Realising that he would not sleep again, he eased himself from the bed. He was not alone in his room. Faces crowded him, his own faces hung upon the wall, in pastel and black ink. From one leaf-face Timon's gaze shone, and the green, laser-thin light of those clear eyes lanced him.

'Be careful,' said Timon's eyes. 'Run, run for home.'

This is my home, thought Daniel, puzzled.

He stepped onto the landing. The nearest he had to a thought was that his teeth needed brushing. His throat was barbed with thirst. An Italian aria shrilled by him as Ruby's hi-fi stretched for a top C, and he shifted past the crack of light at the bottom of her door.

A celebration meal, had Ruby said? Then on somewhere – Max and his mother might be any amount of time. Their room, beyond Ruby's, was drenched in moonlight. Somewhere in there Lisa kept all her letters, diaries – everything from the old days. All that he had not known concerning Timon might be there, if he had the courage to seek it. And he needed to know – now more than ever. At the centre of his life crouched a lie, like a toad at the bottom of a well. Timon was not dead. The different, half-told stories could not fit.

He stood by the door, trailing his nails against the handle. The chill of the metal sang through his fingers, then gave way to something different: wet, slithery, yielding. A strand of fibrous weed hung from him. He shook it off impatiently. In this state he could not think – now, when he most needed to. There was no time. If Timon was real – and Timon *was* real – then someone must have been hiding the truth. What about Timon's own story, of big-time crime, bribes, bodies substituted? That might be true. Daniel had played with such fantasies himself. But hearing Timon he had begun to doubt. Could Timon have been important enough to warrant that much trouble? The more he thought about it, the more it sounded just the kind of glamorous lie Timon specialised in.

He went into Max and Lisa's room. He could have turned the lights on. Ruby was safe, tucked up in an operatic huff; and Aunt Jenkins would be asleep by now, either in bed or dozing through the early-morning reruns on the television. There was little chance of being disturbed. But this was a night-deed, and he left the lights alone.

The obvious places, what were they? The drawers, the back of the big wardrobe. His hand scraped wood, and picked up a splinter. Quickly he moved a chair from the dressing table, took the suitcases from one of the high cupboards, and found them empty. Under the bed was a plain of carpet-fluff tundra. It was only when he lifted one of Lisa's hat boxes that he felt the unnatural weight inside, and set it down with his heart racing again, knowing against reason that it contained what he sought. The box lay in a square of light from one of the lower window panes. On its lid danced a troupe of cherubim, each with wings and trumpet. The lid was fastened with a ribbon in a bow, which he pulled open.

Inside was a jumble of envelopes and papers. Some looked official, with dates stamped on them. One was his own birth certificate. It would take hours to sort through it all, hours he did not have. But here was a piece of luck – a wad of letters and cards, fastened with black ribbon. He pulled out the first envelope and checked the postmark. It was dated six years ago: April the fifth. Just a week after Timon had been found on the beach.

He spread the papers on the floor, and looked at them by the moonlight. Most were greetings cards, a disappointment. How similar all deaths must be, to yield the same phrases so often, the sympathy, the love, the thinking of you at this sad time. Some people had written the words out for themselves, others sent them printed. Everyone was feeling for Lisa, and everyone's sympathy was deep, at this sad time. Daniel saw he had been foolish to expect more. A few wrote of Timon, but it was of his life, not his death: snatches of memory, framed and mounted like one of Aunt Jenkins's photographs – attempts at a likeness. A stranger described how Timon had saved her purse from thieves, thanks to an intrepid rugby tackle. Val's sister remembered that he had left a toffee apple once, on her mother's best chair. There was nothing from Val himself.

Then there was the Reverend Thorpe. He had conducted the funeral service. Daniel remembered his bird-like dipping at the lectern, as he tried to read his sermon without glasses. He skimmed the sympathy, the Christian hope he knew that Lisa did not share. Then he stopped short, seeing his own name. *'It is Daniel who needs you most now.'* The contact gave him a jolt, as though a hand had stretched out and touched him. He had not expected to find his name here – it did not belong. But the Reverend Thorpe had singled him out.

'It is Daniel who needs you most now. They tell me he won't speak of Timon. Perhaps he cannot speak, yet. But when he is ready, then we must all be ready to listen, and listen with loving kindness. The young mind is a complex and mysterious thing. It may be that, in some childish way, he blames himself.'

Daniel reread the letter. He looked at it this way and that, but still it made no sense. He felt cold all of a sudden. Did this clergyman expect him to feel guilty for what had happened to Timon? But that was none of his doing – he had been nowhere near when Timon died. Timon had not involved him, ever. Just once, and that had come to nothing. There had been rumours of drugs: Timon had earned himself a reputation. The police had spoken to him. But Daniel had been only ten years old. It had nothing to do with him ...

Downstairs the front door opened, and Lisa and Max entered, Max talking loudly. The hall light came on, and cast long shadows up the stairs. Startled, Daniel slipped the wad of letters into his pocket, fitted the lid back on the hat box, and tried to reproduce Lisa's neat bow, making a clumsy job of it. He looked around him, at the various pieces of furniture now out of place. There was no time to do anything – he would have to trust to the oblivion of food and drink. Although Lisa was now avoiding alcohol there was something in Max's good humour that spilt into her voice too, tipsily seconding his anecdote with laughter.

'Tolly, is that you?' Aunt Jenkins had stirred from armchair slumber.

'Oh, Aunt Jenkins, are you still up?' asked Lisa solicitously. Max, at the bottom of the stairs, muttered something uncomplimentary as Lisa's voice faded to the living-room. Aunt Jenkins, it appeared, had fallen asleep in front of *Newsnight*, and woken to *Reservoir Dogs*.

'Let's get you to bed,' said Lisa.

'Yes, come on Aunt Jenkins,' said Max, helping. 'Let's get you tucked up nicely.'

Daniel was in his room by the time they made the landing. He turned off his bedside lamp to avoid attention. For ten or fifteen minutes there was a series of footsteps and flushings and door-closings as the three adults put themselves and each other to bed. Ruby was told to keep the noise down. There was silence from her room. Daniel wished she would come back, for he wanted to tell her – and he wanted her to listen to him with loving kindness – to everything he knew about Timon's death. Except that he knew nothing. The Reverend Thorpe had got it so wrong. He felt like crying, because the Reverend Thorpe and everyone had got it wrong. Outside, a fox's scream scratched across the slate-black silence. And nothing again. Nothing disturbed the house, but the unfolding of paper and the click of the lamp, as Daniel took the bundle of letters out and read them through again.

Seven

FOR THE SECOND NIGHT RUNNING, RUBY WOKE TO the knowledge that something in her room had just moved. A sound, sharp but not loud, like the snapping of a dry twig – something like that was responsible. Less alarming than the dream of the crying child: but then that *had* been only a dream. This sound was real, and so was the fluttering presence that hung momentarily about the end of her bed, regarding her as she opened her sleep-meshed eyes. The radio alarm was silent for half a minute, then the red digits on the clock flicked to 8.30, and at once the day hit the ground running. A government minister was discussing what to do with young offenders.

'I hear a lot about the ills of society. But there comes a point when people must stop blaming circumstances, and take responsibility for their own actions.'

'But surely, minister, you were elected on the promise that you would do something to improve—'

Ruby shut it out. The last minute's confusion was already resolving itself into the shape of a Sunday morning at Morton's Holt. Lisa's bathroom sickness was exacerbated today by whatever spiced dish Max (whose tastes ran to the Indonesian) had persuaded her to try. Ruby held the image in her mind without sympathy: Max urging Lisa on, the slur already in his voice, and Lisa's protests increasingly unheard. Death by lime juice, death by lemon grass. But Lisa's actions were her own, the minister was right. And Max was right, whose views were the minister's.

By now she was up and dressing. It might be Sunday, but psychology would not go away. Exams were important: if she could get good grades this summer she would stand a better chance of working with Professor Schliemann the following year. She had her schedule.

But something unscheduled was at her feet. A square of paper lay on the floor in front of her door. She stooped, to find familiar writing on it.

I´VE SEEN TIMON

The paper was a scrawl, written hurriedly. It seemed to have been crumpled up and then smoothed out again, as if Daniel had changed his mind more than once about whether to throw it away. Ruby was suspicious, but this did not feel like a trick. Puzzled, she folded the paper and put it in her pocket.

In the kitchen Lisa was making coffee. Max and Aunt Jenkins sat at opposite ends of a table on which some half-dozen jars of Marmite, jam and honey were set out in patterns. At intervals Aunt Jenkins, dissatisfied with their arrangement, would move one to a new position, with the deliberation of a chess player. Max, behind his newspaper, was trying to ignore this.

'No Daniel?' yawned Ruby at the door, in what she hoped was a nonchalant voice.

'You've missed him,' said Lisa. 'He said something about going to the hide for the morning – took a sandwich.'

'I might join him,' said Ruby, withdrawing.

'What about breakfast?' Lisa called.

Max was deep in the crossword. 'The motherland is going to hell. Nine letters, starts with "D".'

'I'll eat later, OK?'

'I think you should have something – don't you Max?'

'What? Oh yes,' said Max. 'You could use a few extra pounds.'

Ruby stiffened. 'I'm not hungry.'

'Have a cup of coffee at least,' Lisa persisted. 'We hardly see you.'

'Damnation!' Max exclaimed – so loudly that Aunt Jenkins spilt her tea.

Ruby slipped away, leaving Lisa to persuade Aunt Jenkins of the difference between solving a cross-word clue and real swearing. It was a lucky escape. Outside, the air hung faint and still. Ruby breathed deeply, trying to exhale the irritation that Lisa's edgy overtures always produced. Irritation, followed by equally pointless guilt. She followed the path beside the magnolia and the long laurel hedge, which as it entered the wood was invaded by hawthorn and rowan. The hawthorn buds, each a full-fisted pouch of blossom, seemed ripe to burst and snow down on the laurel's sleek scales. Ruby wished she knew the names of all the plants she saw, and envied Daniel briefly. One day she would ask him to teach her.

This part of the wood belonged to the house. Years ago there had been a plan to coppice it, but that had long been abandoned. No doubt the wood did not welcome intrusion. At its centre lay a small lake, which the house deeds called Morton's Pond: a dreary place, with a flotsam of leaves and algae, and banks that crumbled down into dark water. Once, three years before, the pond had floated to land the body of a dog. It was a full-grown labrador, and its lips were curled back, the stick it had leapt in to fetch rigid between its jaws. Lisa had fenced the place round. And nothing nested there, and little grew. From its banks Ruby could see the long slope to Daniel's hide.

The hide was a small lean-to built from doors and an old tarpaulin that Daniel had plundered from a skip when they pulled down some prefabs at school. A pair of school chairs, facing each other, provided him with a seat and a place to rest his legs in the long watching hours. A crate supported pen and notepad. It showed him a long perspective, down to the canal, or east to the bank where badgers lived.

When she reached the hide, Ruby stooped to see if Daniel was inside. At first she could make out nothing, being unused to the shadow of the tarpaulin. She screwed up her nose at the smells, though: of trodden earth, cloth kept too long damp, a sweet decay. The squalor of it depressed her. Daniel kept a thick pottery mug here for tea: she was sure he never washed it.

'You got my message, then?' said a voice beside her. Daniel leaned forward from the shadow. He looked squat and tousled, a sullen Rumpelstiltskin after a hard night spinning straw. Ruby guessed that he had not slept.

'I read it,' she said.

He stared hard at her, daring her to laugh. 'Well?'

'Well, I don't understand it.'

'I've seen Timon,' Daniel said, the intensity ebbing from his face. His scowl flattened out into a kind of bemusement. 'That's what I mean. Timon's not dead after all.'

He seemed to have been distracted by something in the wood, behind her. Ruby felt herself shiver. Glancing back she half-expected to see Timon come floating across the autumn leaves.

'Last night, it was,' said Daniel. His calm was glassy and unreal. 'When I was out, he talked to me. He's been living rough the last six years.'

Ruby sensed she had better tread carefully. 'You mean, he stopped you in the street? Just like that?'

'Yes, more or less. We talked for half a hour. I bought him some food.'

'I see,' said Ruby, beginning to feel out of her depth. Daniel was deadly serious, and this was no joking matter. 'But how did he know you? After this time?'

'He'd been waiting for me,' Daniel said vaguely. 'I think he's been watching the house.' He seemed oddly incurious, nevertheless.

'That's incredible,' Ruby began cautiously.

'It ought to be, I know that. The funny thing is, it's as if I've always known, now. As if I was just waiting for him to turn up. Isn't that strange?'

Ruby remembered the young man in the garden. 'He must have changed a lot,' she said. 'He'd be, what? In his twenties by now.'

Daniel nodded. 'I almost didn't recognise him.'

'No wonder.' Something occurred to Ruby, but it would be hard to put into words. 'Look Daniel – think about it. Think carefully. Can you be sure it *was* Timon?'

The scowl was back. 'You think I wouldn't know my own brother?'

'It's been a long time,' Ruby soothed him. 'People change, and memories change. This person who calls himself Timon. I mean, he may look like him, but—'

'*You – think – I – wouldn't – know – my – own – brother?*'

'They buried him, for crying out loud! They found his body!'

'The body on the beach was some other poor kid. They made it look like it was Timon – he explained it all to me. Timon had to run, and he ran hard for six years.' Daniel had retreated into the tarpaulin. Ruby recognised the signs.

'Oh, Daniel,' sighed Ruby.

He turned sharply. 'What do you mean, "Oh, Daniel"?'

'You want this too much.'

'You're talking rubbish.'

'I know, don't you see? I know how much you loved Timon – how close you were. You'd do anything to see him again.'

Daniel gave a bitter laugh. 'We were never close. He despised me.'

'All the more reason,' insisted Ruby, not to be knocked off her stride. 'You want to make it right this time round. A second chance – a miracle! That's why you've convinced yourself. Or let yourself be convinced.'

'Is this what they teach you in first-year psychology?' asked Daniel rudely.

'Don't get me wrong. I don't think you're having delusions or anything.'

'Thank you, doctor.'

'I mean, if it *is* Timon, then that's great. But why

all the secrecy? Why doesn't he turn up at the front door?'

'Maybe he doesn't fancy the broken nose he'll get when it's slammed in his face. Look at us. Mum's remarried, you're here, and now with the baby it's going to be a full house. No room at the inn.'

'He must know Lisa would never turn him away.'

'He's not a trusting person. But I don't know why I'm talking to *you* about it. You never even met him.'

'I'm only trying to help you, for goodness' sake!' cried Ruby. 'Why'd you write me that note if you didn't want me to say anything?'

'I don't know. Just another of my mistakes.'

Ruby looked at his defiant face, distorted with resentment.

'I guess I just made one of those, too,' she said, letting the tarpaulin fall back across the entrance to the hide. She walked back to the house, and took her books into Max's study. A big mistake, yes – to expect Daniel to change. She'd often tried to approach him, but it always ended this way, or something like it. And now the thought of him, bedded down in his self-pity there in the hide, would spoil her concentration. His cock-and-bull story about Timon distracted her, and so did the thought of Lisa, and the young man who stood waving in the moonlight. She glanced at the calendar, saw how the days were passing. Even this made her anxious, though she longed to leave – why should that be? And all this talk of babies depressed her so.

She felt no better when she wandered to the kitchen, to find Max and Lisa discussing clothes with Aunt Jenkins. Aunt Jenkins had been persuaded to look through some knitting patterns. They were huddled at the kitchen table, with pictures of socks and cardigans spread out before them.

'This one's pretty,' Max ventured. He pointed to a hat with a border of lemon yellow and a fluffy bobble.

'Yes,' Lisa said doubtfully. 'But look, it needs six different colours! Have some pity on Aunt Jenkins!'

'I'm sure Aunt Jenkins can cope. I've seen those fingers whirl.'

'I am allowed my own opinion, I suppose,' said Aunt Jenkins. 'The hat is very well in itself. But what use is a winter hat to a summer baby?'

'It won't be summer for ever, will it?' Lisa pointed out.

'I think it never will be,' Aunt Jenkins commented in a spirit of gloomy self-contradiction. 'But perhaps I had better start by making him a pair of socks.'

'Why does everyone assume that this baby is going to be a boy?' Ruby asked. All three turned round: they had not heard her come in. She leaned her elbows on the back of Aunt Jenkins's chair. 'I think I'm going to have a sister.'

'I don't know where these rumours start,' said Max.

'I suppose it's because I've always produced boys in the past,' said Lisa. 'But if it was a girl—' She hesitated. The fear of expressing a preference had become a superstition with her.

'Yes? What if it was a girl?' prompted Ruby.

'Why, I'd love it. I've always wanted a daughter.'

'A real daughter you mean? Not just a step like me?'

'Ruby,' Max growled.

'You're hardly at the age for plaits, and the rest.

Look at you, you're grown-up. You live away from home – you've got a driving licence!'

'Yes, I know. Much too old to be cute.'

'Don't be obtuse, Ruby,' Max said.

'I think I understand quite well. This is some kind of trip for you, isn't it? You want a baby because it proves you two are for real.'

'"For real!" Is that the way you and your friends talk in Durham?'

'You don't know *what* I do in Durham,' Ruby retaliated.

'I know you do it very largely on my money,' said Max.

Ruby did not reply at first. Then she said, in a different voice: 'Don't worry, I bless you in my prayers each night, Dad. What you give me is enough to keep a roof over my head, and a bed to sleep in. But sometimes I have this urge to eat as well. Why do you think I've been doing bar work for the last two terms?'

'Bar work?' Max was at once ruffled, just as she had wished. 'You never mentioned that.'

'Why should I?' asked Ruby. 'It's my business. And it's only three nights a week.'

'Still, but those late nights …' Max said uncertainly. For the moment at least the baby was forgotten. 'This bar work, it's in the college, I suppose? At the Union?'

'No, in town. One of those new Irish pubs: Reilly's Crack House. Not quite as naff as it sounds. We've even had one or two real Irish in there.'

'What about getting home afterwards?' Max objected. 'A girl on your own, late at night …'

'That is *exactly* why I don't talk to you, Dad!'

Ruby exclaimed, slamming the table. 'The first thing you do is think of objections. What happened to "That's very interesting, Ruby," or "How enterprising, Ruby!" Aren't you pleased I've got a life of my own?'

'Of course I am!'

'Look, I'm eighteen, and I've got my head screwed on. I can vote, I can get married, I can go to parties on my own – and I know how to call a cab. Give me some credit!'

'Max is concerned for you, Ruby,' said Lisa. 'You only need to pick up the paper to see some dreadful story.'

'I don't need any lessons from you, Lisa. You'd already had Timon by the time you were my age, that's how careful you were. I can guess what your parents thought about that – to say nothing of Aunt Jenkins here.' Ruby smiled. On impulse, she decided to take the next step too. 'Oh, did I say about the customers in the Crack House? One of them was a very charming man, from Dublin. An amateur conjurer, fond of whiskey chasers. Sound familiar?'

Lisa's face was expressionless. Aunt Jenkins rose from her chair, and made towards the door. Max, for once, had nothing to say.

'We had a long, long talk,' said Ruby. 'We were surprised to find we had so many friends in common, Valentine and I.'

Lisa was the first to recover. '*You* know Val?'

'I've served him several pints of stout, if that means knowing. I told you, he was a customer.'

'A tricky customer!' said Lisa. 'That won't be all. If he ferreted you out he had something underhand in mind.' She spoke with a bitterness that was sudden and vehement.

'Who said anything about ferreting? It's an Irish pub. He lives in the city and he came in to check it out. It, not me.'

'You're so naïve, Ruby.' Lisa turned away impatiently. Max went to put a hand on her shoulder, but she shook him off. 'Oh, you think the same as her, I know you!' She turned on Ruby once again. 'Just tell me this. Who discovered the family connection, you or him?'

'I don't even remember. He could tell I wasn't a Geordie, so he asked what part of the country I came from. Didn't take long for Morton's Holt to come up. OK?'

'Not OK! Can't you see he's just using you? To get at me?'

'Oh, sorry Lisa, I forgot you were the centre of the universe. Well, believe me, Valentine has moved into a different orbit. He doesn't think about you now.'

'He doesn't forget. And he's got a nasty line in cold revenge.'

'You really are malicious, aren't you?' said Ruby, shaking her head in wonder. 'That's one thing Val's got right.' She went to the kitchen door, turned, and said sweetly to Max: 'Dad, I'm going into town now. I'll be out all day, I expect. All night too, perhaps. Don't wait up. Oh, and don't worry. If I get lost I'll ask a policeman.'

Alone, Max and Lisa found themselves embalmed in a silence as sticky as amber.

'What if Ruby's right?' said Lisa at last. She seemed suddenly subdued.

'Malicious! You?'

'Not that! I mean – why are we having another child after so long?'

'The baby as patch? No, I don't think so.'

'I don't mean that either, quite. But could I be doing this as a kind of *replacement* for Timon? That wouldn't be very fair to either of them.'

'Life isn't that symmetrical, darling. This new one will be his own person, not yours or mine – and certainly not Timon's.'

'Oh, I know we say that. That's how we want it to be most of the time. But what if life's got a pattern after all? What if life pays you back? Timon's been in my thoughts a good deal lately.'

'Don't tell me *you've* seen him looking in the window?'

'It's not funny, Max. Anyway, I'm not the only one. Have you noticed the way Daniel's drawings have changed? He's left off nature spirits and taken to sketching babies. I found a pile of them in the waste-paper bin yesterday, all crumpled up.'

'Babies? That's not so surprising in the circumstances.'

'All those babies had Timon's face, Max.'

Max shook his head. 'That's just Daniel. I thought I'd cured you of reading too much into perfectly explicable events.'

'Then how do you explain *yourself*, Max?'

'What do you mean?'

'You were the one who raised Timon the other night – from nowhere. No one asked you to.'

Max drew himself to his full height. He'd had enough of this. Hindsight was one thing, but picking at scabs was just a dirty habit. 'I've already offered more than one full apology for that. I'm not to blame for what happened to Timon. I've only tried to make your life better, haven't I? Isn't that true?'

'You don't understand what I'm saying,' sighed Lisa.

'What you're saying is just some superstitious yarn, and you're tying yourself in knots with it.'

'Thanks.'

Max took her gently by the arm. 'Lisa, believe me, it's because I love you that I find you so exhausting.'

'Thanks again. That's *so* romantic.'

'Let's not argue over this. Ruby's angry because I've got you. We've always known that, and now with the baby it's worse. This thing with Valentine, it may just be coincidence; but if there was any ferreting going on, let's not assume it was all on his side. Maybe she was looking for a way to get back at us.'

'Well,' said Lisa, 'if she wanted a stick to beat me with she couldn't have chosen better than Val.' She straightened the pile of catalogues. 'But if she wanted him for more than that,' she added, 'then she couldn't have chosen worse.'

Eight

'WAS THAT NICE?' Jane moved her mouth back from his. Her taste was mint, and cherry-glossed lips.

'Was what nice?' asked Daniel.

She laughed, her head to one side. 'Answer the question, you idiot!'

'Yes. Oh yes, it was nice.'

'Good.' She kissed him again, on the cheek. 'Now maybe you'll lighten up a bit.'

'I'm sorry. I don't mean to be this way. I'm getting so I'm scared of my own shadow.' Daniel held his hands out in front of him, to check for the shakes – but the bus was shaking everyone as it was, over the speed bumps and the bad road. Instead he checked his watch, and found that he had just one hour before he was due at Marley's. He felt the warmth of Jane's shoulder against his. This might be a good moment. There might not be a better. 'Do you mind if I ask you something?'

'Of course not. Why should I mind?'

'No reason,' said Daniel.

After a while Daniel said: 'If I said I was falling in love with you, would you be angry?'

Jane squeezed the bag on her lap protectively to her. She did not seem surprised, but nor did she have an answer ready-made. 'I've known that for weeks,' she said at last. 'Why would that make me angry?'

'It might have.' Daniel had been through all the scenarios. 'I'd rather you took it as a compliment.'

'I do. I'm flattered, Daniel. You're very sweet.'

Daniel felt his stomach turn. Sweet. That was a letting-down-gently word. A sickly, puppy-dog word. No girl called you sweet if she took you seriously.

'What's the matter?' asked Jane.

'But you – you don't feel anything?'

She put her hand in his. 'Let's not rush things, OK?'

'OK, let's not.'

She let her eye move up and down the aisle, reading the names on the bags of Saturday shopping. Daniel could see her thinking of a way to change the subject, and wished he had not so impetuously spoiled things. All Jane had wanted was to come into town and spend some money on a top. She'd met him on the bus; playfully she'd kissed him. That ought to have been enough. None of this was her fault.

'I'm buying my step-sister a CD,' he said.

'Oh?'

'A kind of peace offering.'

'Oh.'

'I've been a pig to her lately.'

Jane said: 'What kind of music does she like?'

'Weird modern classical stuff. Sounds like it's being played backwards half the time.'

'She must be clever.'

Jane sounded as if she'd have liked a CD too. But when Daniel snaked his hand further into hers she let it lie, and the silence was not so awkward. The bus was taking a crazy route, between office blocks empty because of the weekend. Nearby was Max's office, and his old flat lay in sight across the harbour, one of the hundred windows speckling the tobacco warehouse. The new Exhibition Centre lay choppily reflected in the harbour water. Nobody got on board until they clipped the shopping streets again. Daniel was fascinated by the way the strands of Jane's hair turned to rainbow prisms in the sun. He was replaying their conversation in his head and listening for grace notes, and noticed only dimly the train of grey figures who washed against the bus at the last waterfront stop. They climbed aboard, their faces hidden and coats trailing the ground with streaks of mud. Someone must have opened a window, for the sound of the gulls was suddenly louder. And talk of the sea was in everyone's mouth.

'The floods they've had up the coast ...'

'Never been such a spring tide.'

'Livestock drowned in the fields.'

He shifted his hand a little deeper into Jane's. She seemed not to notice.

'Strange creatures washed up, they say.'

'All kinds of things ...'

'Daniel, isn't this your stop?' asked Jane, shaking the rainbows from her.

'Yeah,' said Daniel. He saw the driver about to pull away. 'I – I'll catch you later.' Hop-scotching past the other passengers' bags he leapt down to the pavement.

Jane waved from the bus, smiling. He waved back – then something made his hand drop to his side and clutch the hem of his coat.

It was the group of lean figures sitting behind Jane. They were sprawled across the back rows of the bus, with the collars of their long coats turned up. He could not make them out distinctly, for the glass was misted, but he saw how their hair straggled down across their shoulders in rats' tails. Their fingers were sallow grey sticks, and their heads – so supple that they seemed hardly to be attached to their bodies – twisted around and around. In a moment of horror it came to him that these were not real people at all. Their limbs were driftwood, their muscles strung with twists of weed.

He leant his head back against the bus shelter, and took a breath. He knew that what he had just seen was impossible. The muffled passengers were just that – shoppers, wary of the sudden spring chill and wrapped against it. He tried to break the mood by thinking of something ridiculous: knobbly knees, mauve underpants. But looking up he saw a disdainful angel shake a fist at him from the porch of a nearby church, and felt guilty of some monstrous neglect. He was walking by St Michael-on-the-Quay, where the Greek columns hung grandly above tarmac. This road had once been part of the harbour front, before they filled it in two generations back. Ships had moored here, and rich merchants beautified the chapels. Now motor traffic plied and span beside him. And still his thoughts were of a grey sea mist swarming down the aisle between dusty panes, and catching Jane's red hair in its billows.

A large roundabout lay between him and the shopping centre. The only safe way across was through a series of underpasses, leading to a large central well that was open to the sky. There the drunks sat and exchanged the times of day and night, while lorries whirled about them like dirty planets. Daniel hated the place. Usually he would duck under the barriers and dodge four lanes of traffic to avoid it. But today he followed where the railings led – down the strip-lit tunnel, herded with shoppers from the bus rank above.

As he emerged he saw a drunk come towards him, limping. He knew at once that he was not going to escape. The drunk told him that his leg was bad. His leg had been bad for years, but no doctor would see him. Daniel tried to move past, but the man gripped his arm. 'Do you have my bus fare?'

'Where are you going?' Daniel looked at the man's yellow fingers, which were broad and flat and strong.

'How far is it to Eastbury? I have a sister there. She'd put me up, I know she would.'

'You're in the wrong city,' said Daniel. 'There's no such place.'

'Are you trying to be funny?' The grip tightened. The man's eyes were overhung by curls of yellow-grey hair. He was not as old as he had looked at first.

'Look, I'm not trying to be funny. I don't know where Eastbury is.'

'I just need a chance to get back on my feet. I'll pay you back ...' His breath was a cocktail of gin and stale cigarette smoke. It made Daniel want to cough.

'Have a heart, Fuller! Leave the kid alone!'

The words came from one of the underpasses, sixty yards away. They were not shouted, but they pushed aside the traffic's noise, lazily. The drunk released Daniel's arm, and turned back reluctantly to his bench, where two of his companions had been placidly awaiting him. Daniel looked up, to see a man in a cheap jacket and tie. He was bisected by the crisp shadow at the entrance to the underpass. Dark glasses made his smile seem whiter, and he nodded to Daniel as if he knew him. But now Daniel was deflected by a group of women hurrying in convoy from one subway to another, and a small boy on long reins that one of them was tugging behind her.

'Come *on*, Nathaniel!' called the woman, while Daniel flailed to prevent himself from falling over the lagging child. When he looked again the man with the white smile and the dark glasses was gone. Buses and cars were orbiting his head.

He rushed up the far underpass and sat for forty minutes in the precinct, near to Marley's. Ruby's CD would have to wait now: there was something else that couldn't. That man with the dark glasses, the one who had called off Fuller – he had seen him before. It seemed a long time ago, or not so long. A submarine light was beginning to shine on him, a light from below. The underpass, why did he avoid it? What did it have to do with the Reverend Thorpe? A flock of starlings flew down from the pitched roof of the shops opposite and landed at his feet, picking over the ground for food.

It may be that he blames himself. For a week Daniel had puzzled at the phrase, cursed the Reverend Thorpe's pomposity, pulled at a cotton-thin thread of memory only to feel it break in his hands. But now something had happened. He felt his memories grow unfamiliar, and spread within him, and change the shape of him. He was his own accuser. And his own confessor. And he knew what he had done.

He had been ten years old when Timon had whistled from his bedroom window: 'Daniel, I've a job for you.'

Daniel had been collecting beetles on the lawn. Timon smiled at him. It takes all sorts, the smile seemed to say.

'What job?'

'The kind you'll get twenty for if you do it right.'

Daniel went to Timon's room. Timon's ankle was in plaster from an accident at school, and he could get nowhere without crutches. But Timon could not keep still. He'd stand at the window, or try lying on the bed, the floor, then raise himself again. His walkman played on where he had left it near the door, a distant patter of wire brush sound. It might have been his brain whirring.

'You know the underpass by the council offices? Leading up to Hills Road?'

Daniel nodded.

'Then you'll have seen him yourself,' said Timon. 'Most times of the day and night he's there, a guy with a harmonica. Dark glasses to make people think he might be blind. Plays all the blues numbers.'

Daniel nodded again – he thought he knew the man. The underpass was haunted by blues music, and there was a man playing it in the sharp bend near Hills Road. Dirty, like he slept down there. He always *was* there.

Timon put his hand on his shoulder, as if he were about to give him a promotion. 'Good, good,' he said. He hobbled off to the walkman and switched the tape around. The wire brush sound started again.

'I want you to give him this.' Timon opened his drawer, and produced a brown packet.

'What's that?' asked Daniel.

'None of your business. You're just the postman, OK?'

Daniel turned to leave. 'If you don't trust me you can deliver your own letters.'

'Not while I'm like this I can't,' said Timon, tapping his bad ankle on the bedpost. 'Why do you think I'm paying you twenty pounds?'

'It must be important,' said Daniel. He was beginning to enjoy having Timon need to ask him favours. 'Who is this man, anyway?'

A flicker of impatience crossed Timon's face. He moved to the window and looked out, leaning his thin body against the glass as if he had been propped there. 'If you must know,' he said, 'he's a friend of Dad's.'

'Dad's!' Daniel exclaimed. They had heard nothing of Valentine since he had left five months before.

'He's one of Dad's old drinking mates. He knows where he is, and he'll tell us – at a price.'

Daniel followed his brother's gaze to the envelope. He remembered how the police had been round in a squad car, talking about drugs. Lisa had cried all night. 'He knows I know people,' said Timon. 'I made a deal.'

'I won't do it.'

'Not for twenty pounds?'

'Not for any money.'

He met Timon's eye, but clear as glass his brother's own shone back. 'I should have expected that from you. You always were a coward.'

'I'm not!'

'And selfish with it.'

'I don't like drugs, that's all.'

'Who mentioned drugs?' cried Timon indignantly. 'You've got a nerve. Just think about it, Daniel. This guy is the only link we've got to Dad. Mum doesn't know where he is – you can see it's doing her head in. This family's going down the pan, and all you can do is whinge.' He tossed the packet back into the drawer. 'It's pathetic.'

'Hang on a minute,' Daniel protested. He knew that Timon was the one with the nerve – who never acted in anyone's interests but his own. But in the face of his brother's fierce assurance his own reason cowered, and the words to frame it fled.

'You still here?' asked Timon aggressively. 'Go on,

get back to your four-leaf clovers, or whatever it is you really care about.'

'If this man did tell you where Dad was ...' Daniel began.

'Yes?'

'Do you think we could persuade him to come back?'

Timon gave a snort, and clapped his hands to show how sure he was. 'This woman he's gone off with, I've seen her picture. She's about fifty, she's got a squint. She won't keep him. Not a man like Dad.'

Downstairs the front door closed. Lisa was walking the gravel drive.

'You do *want* to see our dad again, don't you?' said Timon. 'You want to see Mum happy?'

'You know I do.'

'Well then.'

Well then. That was six years ago. And wherever Lisa's happiness lay, Daniel knew better now than to think it was in the gift of Valentine.

As for the man with the harmonica and dark glasses, that was another story.

Daniel worked hard at Marley's, and Mrs Kinsale showed her appreciation with a share of the tips. She slipped an extra fiver into his coat pocket as he was getting ready to go. 'There's no reason,' she said, 'why our back-room boy should go without.'

'Thanks, Mrs Kinsale.'

'And you're sure you can do some extra days this week, while I'm short-staffed? Good lad. Give my love to your mother, won't you?'

'I will, I will,' said Daniel.

'See you, Daniel,' chorused the three waitresses as the door tinkled open. In scarves and sensible coats they left the shop together, talking comfortably of the latest epidemic.

Daniel took off his apron and hung it up, swapping it for his own thick coat. He felt the need of it as soon as he left the tearooms, for the air outside was harsh. Mrs Kinsale was in the back office as he left, so she did not see the crouched figure who waited for her washer-up in the turning of the street outside, nor hear how with a whistle Daniel was diverted from his normal path and greeted, and led towards the place where the sea was briefly visible between tall cliffs of brick. There the engines choked, their treble lost to the bass of the sea's breathing. So close was the city to that wide world of water, and so far, that when Daniel looked back the streets seemed already faded to a great remove, shrouded by the sea mist. Had he not been a native of this place he might not have known how to return. Timon was walking beside him.

'It's good to see you again,' said Daniel.

'That's lucky. I'll be here for a while, I hope.'

'Where are we going?'

'Somewhere we can talk without interruption.'

They had come to a meeting of concrete, sea and stone, a yard between warehouses on the edge of the docks. A rope as thick as Daniel's leg lay coiled about a nearby capstan: everything here was on a giant scale. Chains and hooks, made to land a ship with; unfathomable structures surrounded them.

Timon wore a greatcoat now, to which the sea mist clung stickily. He mounted the capstan, and sat cross-legged on it. Perhaps he was trying to look like the Buddha, or a caterpillar on a mushroom. The absurdity of the thought did something to dispel Daniel's nervousness. It occurred to him that the gloom of the place gave Timon a kind of thrill: that he was playing ghosts with him, as he had years ago in the cobwebby cellar of Morton's Holt.

'You've doubted me,' said Timon, mind-reading. He spoke without reproach.

'I've been doubting myself,' said Daniel. 'All that's happened – I thought maybe I was going mad.'

'It amounts to the same thing. Don't let it bother you.' Timon threw a stone, and Daniel heard it splash somewhere in the dark below. He had not thought they were so near the water's edge.

Daniel had meant to lead up to it subtly, but found himself asking: 'So what you told me the other night, about why you ran away. That was all true?'

'It was true in essence. You can't ask for more, not when the details are so painful. You've got something to say?'

'These – people, the ones you were mixed up with. They wanted you out of the way. Why? What exactly had you done to them?'

'Now you're asking.'

'Because I need to.'

'These are deep waters, still.' Timon let the mist curl around his wagging finger.

Daniel heard himself ask: 'Was it because of me?'

Timon's face was the only part of him visible. His body, his sagging greatcoat, were without distinction. There was a soundless flapping nearby that fanned Daniel's skin, as though a sea bird were launching itself into the thick air, and for a moment Daniel lost all sense of his brother's presence.

'Timon? Are you there?'

'Right as rain,' said Timon, but his voice had shifted nearer the water. 'And really there's no need to worry.

In my position, you soon get a sense of perspective.'
There was Timon, teetering along the kerbs above the sea.

'Once – you remember – you asked me to deliver something for you. And I didn't do it.'

'I told you not to worry about it.'

'I just want to know if I'm right. That packet, I never delivered it. I meant to, but I got scared. There were police cars about. Everybody seemed to be looking at me. I thought they could see right through my coat to where those pills were.'

'So you took a peek then? You know what curiosity did, I suppose?'

'The packet was full of pills – there must have been hundreds of them. More than anyone would need for themselves.'

'And you decided to take a moral stand,' said Timon tartly.

'I panicked. When I got to the underpass the guy with the harmonica was talking to two men. They were arguing – I thought they were going to fight. I just ran – I chucked the packet into the harbour.'

'The harbour? I bet the fish were celebrating *that* night. Anything else you forgot to tell me at the time?'

'I just know, it was a couple of weeks later that—'

'That I did my moonlit flit. And you naturally see a connection.'

'I hadn't thought about it for years, till today.'

'Quiet!' Abruptly Timon grabbed his hand and pulled him back into the shadow. His fingers were ice. Daniel found himself being slammed into a wall, the breath knocked from him. He gasped out in surprise, but again Timon silenced him.

'Shut up! It's the Lockermen!'

'The what?'

'The Lockermen – the Night Watch! Shut up!'

Then Daniel saw them. Soundlessly across the wet concrete they came, walking in file. Five, or half a dozen of them, all dressed alike in long, ground-trailing coats. Above their heads darted two little points of light, which illuminated them in flashes. These were lanterns, jerked from the end of pliant, nodding poles. As they came near, Daniel could see their faces – or what passed for faces. He felt a chill to match the pressure of Timon's hand. On their white skin, taut as a balloon's skin, human features were only sketched. Eyebrows, nose and mouth were no more than smudges, flat as pencil lines. Perhaps they were wearing Hallowe'en gear. But then the nearest of them stopped short, and the whole line stopped. By the light of the two lamps Daniel saw six white faces sniff the air, painted nostrils flaring; and six pairs of grey eyes flit from side to side. Cold, pitiless eyes! It was then that he saw the dark shape struggling at the centre of the line. He took it for a dog, or a fox, before he realised it was a boy, a little younger than himself. With increasing desperation he was trying to free himself, but the wilder his movements became the less difference they made. The nearest of the Lockermen held him easily by the scruff of his neck.

'Who is that?' whispered Daniel, petrified.

Timon did not want to answer, but said at last: 'A runaway, like me. Now shut it, or we'll be joining him.' His fingers were hard as stones.

The Lockermen were twisting their balloon heads about. Daniel wished the sea mist would swallow him up, prayed his heart would stop beating. Anything rather than be in the power of those creatures. There was a long wait. Then, at an invisible signal, the Lockermen moved on. They resumed their silent progress towards the wharf's edge. For the first time one of their darting lanterns lit up the face of their victim, and Daniel recognised him. It was the boy he had met the week before, the one he had given money outside the arts cinema. But now his face was white: not just scared but bleached, sucked quite dry. And his body, though it still writhed, was thinner, like a banner flapping. His cries were soundless: they landed in the waiting silence and made no ripple.

As the Lockermen passed, Daniel felt a low wind following. In it were carried all the stenches of the sea, and it opened a tunnel through the mist that led to utter blackness. They must be close to the wharf's edge now. Daniel bit his lip as they silently overstepped it. The first of the Lockermen dropped from sight, then the second. Next came the figure in whose gloved hand the runaway boy rippled like a flag. He too stepped off the wharf: they too were swallowed. The only sound was the hiss of the lamps as the cold water pinched them out.

Somewhere in the outer harbour a fog-horn sounded. Daniel felt Timon's fingers slip from his own, and the movement woke him from a paralysis of horror. He looked at his brother, and realised that he was moving away.

'Timon? Where are you going?'

'Too dangerous …' Timon seemed breathless. 'Can't talk here. There are others.' He backed away, staggering as if the ground were moving beneath him. *'They'll all come now.'*

'Where are you going?' yelped Daniel, in a voice that the mist baffled and lost. 'You're not leaving me!'

'I can't stay. Go back to the lighted streets – it's not you they're looking for.'

'But I don't know where to go …'

'I'll find you again. Soon …'

'Timon?'

'You'll see …'

Timon was thirty yards away now, a forked shadow of darker mist against the firefly speck of a distant floodlight. Daniel chased after, terrified at finding himself alone, heedless of the tell-tale slap of his soles on the wet ground. But as he approached the angle changed, and he saw that what he had taken for his brother was a flag pole, and the horizontal bar of a fence running behind it. Timon, if he had ever been here at all, was gone.

Daniel pulled himself up short. *If he had ever been here?* The thought whispered itself before he had a chance to stop it. Wasn't that what Ruby had been hinting at – that he was seeing things? Perhaps she was right. After what had just happened he even hoped so. But Timon's warning had left him helpless with fright. *They'll all come now.* On every side the mist pressed his skin. He heard the sea run its tongue along the wall of the quay close by. The fog-horn sounded again, and the low sky returned an echo. The sound came in disguise, its direction blunted, but it gave Daniel a bearing. He recognised the silhouette of a gantry, metal containers, a hook and chain angling patiently. The old tobacco dock: he knew where he was, just minutes from the tearooms. He had known it all his life; if the mist had not thrown a glamour over it.

He returned quickly to the streets, and took the long way to the bus station, sticking to the main roads. There, in twos and threes, he found a residue of people standing, while the buses shunted and turned, and the mist dripped from their trembling sides. The lame man from the roundabout was there, nursing a polystyrene cup, but he did not recognise Daniel: he was wrapped in his own vision of Eastbury, and the sister who would put him up if he could get there. Drivers chatted, shouted insults across the forecourt. Daniel sat next to two girls of his own age, and eavesdropped on their conversation. A few names he recognised, the tall and slicked-back pick of his year, whose merits were now analysed casually between sips of hot chocolate. School, where he would find himself in a week's time, seemed like a fairy-tale. Did he belong there? He could hardly remember it. Even Jane Garfield was for the moment a character from someone else's story. He had left the dark, but the mist, and what the mist and the spring tide had brought, remained to haunt him. The city was flooded with his ghost-dream, and all their lives were bobbing on the surface of it.

Nine

R UBY SURPRISED HERSELF BY DISCOVERING THAT her feelings for Lisa had changed. Without any obvious reason, in recent days the tension between them seemed to have slackened. It wasn't that Lisa was behaving any differently. The alteration was in Ruby herself. Not a conversion, more a shifting of weight in Lisa's direction, a permission to relax. Enough at least to prevent her automatically stiffening when Lisa came into a room.

It was the day before Max's birthday that she first became aware of it. Lisa, always striving to turn mere events into occasions, had wanted to mark it grandly. But Max had resisted, and worn her down till all that remained of her celebration was a family tea, with cake. The cake was Aunt Jenkins' idea.

Already things had begun to go a little wrong. Daniel had not turned up, despite promises. Mrs Kinsale had offered him extra work through Easter week, and he seemed to have become incapable of catching a bus back on time. Max was fidgety and not bothering to hide his wish for the rite to be over. Lisa was tense with the desire for Max to be pleased, to appreciate and praise. But as Max was putting the cake to his lips he noticed something.

'You didn't put almond essence in this, did you?'

'A little – why?'

'Lisa, you know I'm allergic to almonds. They don't agree with me at all.' He put the cake back on the plate, where the icing dislodged itself and sank lopsidedly. Lisa watched its glacial descent with a kind of fascination.

'I'm sorry,' Lisa said quietly.

'I'm sure I've mentioned it before.'

'I'm sorry,' said Lisa. Her voice had a quiver in it.

'It's nothing to get upset about,' said Max blithely. 'But I'd have thought you'd have remembered. Ever since that fiasco in the Black Forest ...'

'That was before Lisa's time, Dad,' said Ruby with a sharp stab of the knuckle into Max's thigh.

'I'll make you another one, without almond essence,' said Lisa. For some reason, she was almost in tears. 'I'll make you a cake without any kind of essence.'

Max was bewildered. 'There's no need for that. I'm sure this won't go to waste – it looks wonderful. Won't you try a piece, Aunt Jenkins?' And he launched himself into a round of slicing cake and passing it round on plates with maroon paper napkins.

Ruby could see every thought that propelled her father: it was depressing. The story of the Black Forest, for instance, would have been a joke against himself. Max, in his almond-induced anguish, had forgotten the German for toilet and ended by stumbling out to find relief amongst the resinous pines. He would have told the sorry tale with skill, and perhaps made Lisa laugh. Anything to make her laugh. But what had made her unhappy in the first place, Max would not want to know.

'Ruby, do you know where Daniel has got to? He

swore he'd be back for Max's tea.' Lisa was talking to her, the wobble gone from her voice, or filtered at least through a mouthful of sponge.

'He'll be here. You know he's often late from the café.'

'I asked him specially today. I wanted everything to be – you know – *right*.'

Lisa put her hand across her belly, and closed her eyes as though she were making a wish. She sounded so forlorn, so full of hopes and disappointments. Normally, Ruby would have been irritated; today, she found herself looking at Lisa with a new feeling. It was not pity. Rather, it was a kind of shame. Out of them all, it was Lisa who tried to make things better, to build a family from the unpromising material available at Morton's Holt. Perhaps it was hopeless. Ruby had always thought so: that was why she planned to get her degree and leave for good. But just now her glorious escape seemed cowardly. At any rate she wanted to make things better for Lisa, if she could.

'You know Daniel. He loses track, sometimes, but he won't let you down. Not if he said.'

On cue, Daniel now arrived. His jacket was slung onto the chair in the hall, and the muffled thud of his trainers led to the living-room. A moment later he was with them.

'And where have you been?'

Daniel stood behind his mother, and put his arms around her neck. 'I'm sorry I'm late,' he said. 'Mrs Kinsale wanted me to help tidy the place. And then the buses …'

Lisa's eyes were shut, her cheeks cupped in his hands.

'Your fingers are cold.'

'It's bitter,' said Daniel. His fingertips still tingled from contact with Timon, whom he had just left. Each fibre of his coat was pin-headed with night dew, and stiff with the raw, salt smell he was beginning to associate with those meetings. Outside he had hardly noticed, but in the living-room (already stuffy from the gas fire) he seemed to be pawing aside great swabs of cold air.

'*You* like my sponge cake, don't you?' asked Lisa.

'I live for it.'

But Daniel barely touched the piece she cut him. Ruby watched the way his eyes skated the expressions of Max and Aunt Jenkins. When he spoke it was with polite, bland phrases, the least he could get away with. With his nail he tracked the deceptive pattern on the plate in front of him. Ruby tried to catch his eye, but failed, and after ten minutes he found an excuse to slip away.

It was becoming a regular meeting. After work at Marley's Daniel would stay in town, or dawdle home by untried routes. He found parts of the city he had never known: a park with swings, tower-block lego-lands; sometimes the last canal lock before the water turned brackish in the sea dock. There was a keeper's house there, with coal-black boards striping the window and a Keep Out sign 'By Order'. It did not matter where he went: Timon would find him. It quickly ceased to bother him how Timon knew where he would be. Once or twice he had tried to catch him out – doubling back on himself, spinning unexpectedly to find Timon following. But such tricks were useless. Besides, Timon always seemed to have arrived before him, to have been waiting in fact for some time. Often a pile of cigarette stubs at his feet would testify to his impatience.

On this day Daniel had followed the railway for a mile, on the cycle path that ran beside it, up and out of the city. Occasionally a cyclist would whisk past in a helmet. Then a plastic sheet flapping from the terraced allotments billowed out to show his brother's grinning face, playing scarecrow to a radish patch. A scramble down the stony slope, and Timon dropped beside him.

'You haunt such lonely places, Daniel.'

Timon had changed. Some kind of gel had raised his hair in spikes, giving him the look of a delinquent hedgehog. He wore a pair of new trainers.

'Where'd you get them?' asked Daniel.

'A friend,' said Timon, glancing at his feet in mild surprise. 'He got picked up. I guess you could say I inherited them.'

'Picked up?'

'Yeah, for some petty misdemeanour. Life stinks, eh? Luckily he took my shoe size.' Timon stretched out the toe of one foot, complacently admiring the style. It wasn't an act: whatever had happened to the shoe's first owner was a matter of indifference.

'And the jacket? And the hair?'

'Ah, now you're asking. How unlike you to take an interest. The jacket's his too, as a matter of fact – I don't think he'll be needing it again. But as for the new haircut, that's my own idea. We all need a change now and again, don't you think? Or we get stale, and sad.'

Timon's expression as he said this suggested that Daniel looked stale and sad himself. But Daniel had no wish for a new style: it seemed a kind of disloyalty to change.

They talked, as ever, warily. Neither mentioned the Lockermen.

'You must tell me,' said Timon as they walked along the path. 'Tell me about Mum's new husband. I want to know everything.'

Daniel tried to describe Max. There were various Maxes to choose from. One was the jolly stranger who had appeared at breakfast two years ago, waving his spoon in the sun and crying: 'Won't you join me, Daniel, for the best meal of the day?' Max the prat. That was the first time Daniel had seen him. Lisa, standing in the kitchen doorway with a boiled egg, had winced, knowing from the start that Max had got Daniel all wrong. But there were other Maxes. There was the businessman whose dockside office had twenty feet of uninterrupted glass from which to view the city, a colour fax, a leather sofa: a successful Max who won Daniel's reluctant admiration. Finally there was Ruby's Max, whom Daniel had never met. This Max had watched his first wife die, slowly, of cancer, five years before. This Max knew that beneath the blaring notes of his success there was always another note, low like the drone of a pipe. It was not loud, but it did not go away, and if you listened to it it made the other notes sound thin and shrill, and falsely bright. It was that Max, Daniel thought, whom Lisa loved.

Timon was getting bored with this explanation.

'And there's a daughter? What's her name?'

'Ruby. She's all right. Of course, sometimes she's too—'

'Yes?'

'Nothing. She's good, Ruby. I like her.' Something a little too eager in Timon's question made Daniel back off from what he had been going to say. For his friends at school he had litany of moans about Ruby. She was a swot, a prig, a preener of her own self-satisfied feathers. She was a Daddy's girl. Rehearsing them should have relieved his feelings. More often he felt dissatisfied with himself, small and petty. It was the same malice he now saw reflected in Timon's face. 'I think she'd be there,' he said, 'if I ever needed her.'

'Seems the girl's a saint,' said Timon acidly.

'I never said that.'

'And you're luckier than some. Come on, let's walk: I can feel my veins congealing.'

They continued along the path, where the blackberry bushes leant in over the tarmac, and the potholes waited to hobble careless cyclists. Timon was full of talk, glibly eloquent on the people they saw, and on the life lived beyond the terrace-back's drooping net curtains. He seemed sure of everything except himself; but on that subject was subdued to the point of silence. He turned Daniel's questions aside with a joke, or with some counter-question about life at Morton's Holt.

'I suppose Max will have some impressive hi-fi,' he speculated.

'He does. There's a thirty-inch TV now, and speakers in every corner.'

'He looks the type.'

Daniel glanced at his brother sharply. 'You've seen him?'

A pebble went flying into the grassy verge from the toe of Timon's new trainers.

'I followed him, once, from his office,' he explained. 'I was curious. Expensive suit, Italian briefcase. The car, too – very swish. "This," I said, "is not a man to deny himself the odd material luxury."'

Daniel was not satisfied. 'How did you know where he worked?'

Timon turned to him impatiently. 'Give me a break, Daniel! I talk to people, all right? What do you think I do all day? For a fag, or a swig, or a tab, you can know anything. There's nothing secret in this city.'

'Nothing except you.'

Timon raised an eyebrow. 'I have to be close. I told you what happened. I'm not meant to be here at all.'

Daniel saw an opportunity. 'But that's over, isn't it? You've come back?'

'You don't understand,' said Timon with a kind of tired pity. 'Six years ago I was given a one-way ticket. If they find me here, I'll be history. History for real, this time.' He laid his hand on a post at the bottom of a footbridge. It was a pale, long-fingered hand, with a delta of violet veins. The half-word *Home*, tattooed letter by letter on its fingers, blushed like a wound. 'They don't forget.'

'Then you should go before they find out.' Daniel had suddenly made his mind up about something. 'Timon, you've got to let me tell Mum about you. You're right about Max – he has got money. If she tells him to, I know he'd set you up, get you a new identity or something. He'd find you a flat in another city. People do that, don't they?'

Timon slid his fingers down the post, as if they could find no place to cling there. 'A new identity. Yes, that would be nice. Why do you think I've got these new threads? They're not just a tribute to my exquisite taste. They're the start of a whole new me.'

'Let Max help you then. A silly haircut isn't going to fool anyone for long.'

'You don't understand. I can't leave here.'

'Why not?'

'I've got things to do. I'm on borrowed time already.'

'What things?'

'Things to undo, I should say.' Timon smiled and huffed out a misty breath, which implied sufficiently that nothing Daniel could say would help. 'My business,' he added. 'I'm not getting you involved.'

'You're my brother,' retorted Daniel. 'I'm involved already.'

But as the mist from Timon's breath cleared, he found that the track was an empty hollow, and that his words had gone unheard.

'Tell me, Lisa. Tell me about Timon.'

'It's not a secret, Ruby. He died. It was a tragedy. I don't know if I'll ever get over it properly. I think one never does.'

Ruby nodded, but this was not the answer she was looking for. It led the wrong way – away from Timon himself to Lisa and her grief, to all grief, anyone's. Lisa was not being evasive. But there were places in her mind she stepped around quite unconsciously – immovable furniture. Ruby glanced at the armchair, where Aunt Jenkins' cigarette ash was creeping up towards her twitching finger. Whether Aunt Jenkins was awake or asleep she could not tell: it was a matter of degree. She was like Lisa, but the furniture had piled up higher and blocked out all her light. Would Ruby herself end up that way, if the wrong things happened to her?

Had they happened already?

At that the face of the man in the night-garden flashed into her thought, moonlit and smiling. At the time, she had not recognized him, had hardly seen him.

But in these last days his features had grown familiar, developed like a photographic plate. They were the same ones she recognised from Lisa's mantelpiece and from Aunt Jenkins's album, the crazy pictures Daniel daubed in his room. Timon, with catkins for hair, had saluted her that evening. Timon, who was six years dead.

'But what was he *like*?' she asked. Lisa had stooped to clean the inside of the oven. Ruby saw her shoulders tense but there was no pause as she answered, 'A charmer, like his dad.'

'I wish I could have met him,' said Ruby, surprising herself.

'If you met Val, you could say you've met Timon too. People always said they were like twins, with a 25-year gap. Charmers, both of them.' The way Lisa used it, the word was not a compliment.

'Yes,' said Ruby. 'I know.' Then she added recklessly: 'Lisa, about Val. I think I should tell you. He was more than just a good customer. We – we've seen each other quite a bit.'

Lisa grunted as she squatted beside the hob. 'I guessed that much from the start.'

'I mean, *quite* a bit. In fact—'

Suddenly Lisa was on her feet. 'Val's a cruel man, that's the truth. Deceitful, vain, cruel in body and spirit.' She slammed the oven door as if it had done her an injury. 'Ruby, I've tried not to be bitter, I really have, but to this day I sometimes wish him dead.'

Ten

*T*HE SUN LEANT DOWN ON THE POISED DAY, AND tipped it. A furtive heat was curling itself on Daniel's skin. In the low ditches, where the fallen leaves had banked up a store of moisture, there were new, startling shoots, and a shimmer of warmth which in the smallest breeze was lost. The jersey under his coat seemed too thick after all, even for sitting. He took it off, and hung it from a branch behind his head to shade the drawing-pad.

Daniel had come to the hide intending to sketch the pond. The faint fluorescence of its floating weeds was a challenge, and its stillness so unlike the stillness of paper. He toyed with the subject; but soon found his pencil trailing to the side of the page to play word games with Jane Garfield's name. In some cultures, he knew, names were believed to hold magical powers, to be vessels of the soul itself. Power over the name was power over the person: power to summon, power to enforce. Daniel was above sticking pins in dolls; but the letters of a name could be tortured almost blamelessly, and somewhere, by some sympathetic power, Jane might respond. Who knew what might come of it?

Jane Garfield yielded various anagrams. FADING RAJ EEL, he wrote. The image slithered through his mind: a down-at-heel, Anglo-Indian fish. Useless – and JAIL-

FED ANGER was no better. The paper fluttered to the ground next to the hide, where the leaves from the previous autumn had swirled in, and begun to form a delicate mulch. In time the paper and its anagrams would break down too. Every molecule would undergo a transformation, feeding a lichen, or churning in the belly of a worm. Nature would make its own anagrams of his ingenuity. He felt the process physically, the slow drip-feed of power from his fingers, sucked from his pen and put to other uses.

It was always like this after seeing Timon. He would come away feeling charged, but with an energy that radiated from him uselessly. He was a red-hot angry little bullet, flying through space. It was frustrating, addictive. He looked down at his voodoo anagrams. Magic. The word hovered over much of what had been happening in these last weeks. But for Daniel magic had all the wrong associations: it made him think of children's parties, of rabbits and knotted handkerchiefs, and of his father. Nothing to do with life. Standing on the hillock beside the hide, he saw the faint gleam of the canal water pinking the branches. Not long before, he had made his early-morning escape there with his fishing rod, but his world was no longer the same thing at all. When he looked back at those weeks, he seemed to be peering down the wrong end of a telescope, to be watching events with a terrible, inconsequential clarity.

He returned to the house. Crossing the lawn, he saw the French windows of the conservatory flung open, and Ruby and his mother inside. Lisa was laughing at a joke Ruby had made, which Daniel couldn't quite hear. He recognised the teasing note in her reply, though. Ruby span the watering can round and gave Lisa a sprinkling, at which Lisa screamed in mock-outrage: 'You menace! I'm not meant to have shocks like that!'

'You were the one wishing we had a shower,' grinned Ruby. 'Oh, here comes someone else who could do with a wash.'

'Watch out, Daniel, she's lethal!'

'Behind the ears, that's where you need it, Daniel.'

Daniel smiled at them vaguely and hurried through into the dining-room, where Max was staring at his laptop as if at a cocked pistol. Max was finding it hard to concentrate with the noise, and conveyed as much by a series of tuttings and sighs. His forehead glowed, up to the sudden border of cropped brown hair. The screen showed a list of figures in one corner, and a pair of purple dolphins disporting themselves in the general shape of a yin-yang symbol – or was it perhaps a tennis ball? Daniel felt one of his occasional spasms of curiosity about Max's business, but resisted the urge to ask questions with long answers. He had his own project.

He went to his room, to the three short shelves of books that had accumulated over the years. There were not many safe hiding-places in this house. Occasionally Lisa would take a bin bag and run round culling items judged to be outworn or outgrown. Loaded with toys, books and clothing, the bag would find its way to the nearest charity shop, and for half a day she would float exultantly through her newly-spacious home. Though Daniel protested, he knew what drove her to it. It was the same thing that stopped her turning Timon's room into a shrine. It was an act of faith, in a future where she could walk forward gleaming and unencumbered, having sloughed off the past like a dead skin. But of course the past called her back too, ceaselessly. It called in many voices. It seemed to Daniel that one of the voices was his own.

On the top shelf stood the eight volumes of the *Children's World of Wonders*. This was one possession whose loss Daniel would have borne happily, but respect for education had prevented his mother from touching it at any time in the eight years since an enthusiastic uncle had given him it as a birthday present. Daniel knew this, and its advantage. He pulled down Volume Two, and turned to the article on Banking. Two ten-pound notes fluttered to his feet. His first pay packet: Timon had presented them, along with a grunt of thanks, on his return from the errand to the Harmonica Man. 'And don't go flashing it around,' he added. 'Mum will get suspicious if she sees you've got cash all of a sudden.'

Daniel had not been able to spend it anyway. It was money he had not earned. When Timon had finally hobbled downstairs to the telephone he had taken the notes and held them to the light: they were greasy, scribbled all over with figures and hieroglyphs. They knew more than he did. Leaning over the banister he heard his brother discussing him.

'Yeah, my kid brother. Yeah, cute as a button. Two hundred, no problem. Next month? Course I'm on for it. Relax, it's sorted.'

He had felt sick, with the giddy feeling that he always had when Timon tricked him. 'Just one more push, Daniel, a gentle one.' Val was not coming home. The Harmonica Man was no friend of his – that was just a line Timon had dangled for him. But this time he had tricked Timon back. It wasn't sorted: the packet was at the bottom of the harbour. The thought of that gave him a secret pleasure.

The money had been hidden in the *World of Wonders* all that time. And now at last he needed it. Twenty pounds, plus what he had earned at Marley's the previous day, would just cover the cost of a silver chain. Besides, he wanted to be rid of that money. The grubby brown paper, with its scribbled runes, seemed like a bad luck charm.

Jane held the chain up to her neck, admiring it on herself.

'It's lovely. Oh, but Daniel – I can't take this.'

'Why not?'

'It must have cost too much.'

'It's my money. I want you to have it.'

Jane gazed at the chain and dangled it from her finger with a kind of wistful regret; then handed it back. 'It's not just the money.'

'What, then?'

She seemed to be thinking of a tactful way to say something. But apparently there was none. 'My Dad's warned me off.'

'He's *what*?'

'He's said I'm not to see you.'

This sounded so prim that Daniel laughed. 'Why? Does he think I'm going to spit on the carpet?'

'Don't be silly,' Jane said irritably. They had reached the corner of her road, where there was a pillar box. She edged around it, putting the box between them. 'It's not like that.'

'No? What's it like?'

'He didn't say anything that specific. Just told me – you know – there were still things he knew more about than me. He said you were bad news.'

'And?'

'And what?' Jane repeated, dully.

'And what did you say to him? That it was none of his business?'

She wouldn't meet his eye. 'I don't know. Maybe he's right.'

'Oh, this is wonderful!' Daniel started to throttle the nearest gate post.

'It's not that I don't care for you, Daniel. But there's something about you that seems – well, *doomed*. It's like an aura you give off. I can't explain it any better than that. It scares me.'

It was hard for Daniel to speak. She was talking nonsense, but it was the kind of nonsense he already half-believed.

'Then there's nothing I can do about it,' he said. 'I've got a skeleton in my cupboard, a dead brother – I smell of mortality! What a wonderful human being your father is.'

Jane added: 'He and Mum are friends with Gabriel's parents.'

'I bet they are!' laughed Daniel.

'That's in it somewhere. They like to matchmake.'

'What – you and Gabriel?'

'They were cut up about it when we finished last time. You'd think it was an arranged marriage. They're old army mates, you see, my dad and his. Gabriel wants to join too.'

'And you're down to be an army wife?'

'If he had his way. Probably.'

'You'll be taking his advice there too no doubt,' said Daniel.

'Don't start on that,' said Jane. 'Gabriel's history, you know it.'

'History repeats itself.'

'You're not even close to being funny.'

'I'm not trying to be.'

Suddenly she turned on him. 'I think you never were funny. Just bitter, and sad, and a bit pathetic.'

Daniel couldn't say anything. He could only watch Jane's mouth as it shaped the words. 'I tried to be nice to you, and suddenly it's like you're hanging round every corner. You're creepy, Daniel, do you get that?'

'I haven't been hanging round!'

'Oh, no!' Jane hooted. 'This is the boy who trailed me home from school!'

'Once! It was the first time I'd even seen your house.'

'So it wasn't you my mum saw nosing about our back yard last night? She almost called the police.'

'Of course it wasn't me! I don't know what your mum's seen.' He felt the veins bulging in his temple: his blood raced, even as his mind reeled back. He stared across the silence that lay between them. 'Jane, you do believe me, don't you?'

'I don't know what you want of me, Daniel. I don't know what space you want me to fill inside your head. But you've never even tried to get to know *me*, have you? I mean *me*, for *my* sake?'

'That's not true!'

'I think it's arrogance. Oh you're very quiet, but it's because you're waiting for everyone to notice how marvellous you are. It's like you're testing them. At least when Gabriel shows off it's plain to see. He's more honest than you.'

Daniel shook his head.

'Well, it doesn't matter,' she said. 'If we'd ever been together I'd be telling you now that we were finished. As it is – I don't want to see you, OK?'

That was it. They were at the entrance to Jane's cul-de-sac. Daniel could have walked to her door and argued, until perhaps the venetian blinds had been pulled up and one of her parents sallied out to snatch her away. Or he could do what he did, and watch her run back home without offering a word to stop her. He could not trust himself to speak.

He posted the chain through the pillar box's astonished mouth. His own mouth felt as if it would never open again.

'It was you who answered yesterday, wasn't it? Yeah, I'd know the sound of your breathing anywhere. You got my letter, Val? But I sent it four days ago!' Ruby looked at the calendar above the hall table. 'No, listen, that doesn't matter. What I wrote before – I wasn't sure then, but it's getting beyond wishful thinking. Yes, yes of course, what other father could there be? Val, wait!' She put her hand to her brow, trying to find a way to say it. 'Can you come down? I need you. There's been some things happening – things to do with Daniel. Timon too in a way. Yes, I know what you said. A clean slate – but you've got to take some respon— Val? Val? You can't just run away, Val!'

But Val had hung up.

Ruby put the phone back on the hook and swore.

On the bank beside the hide, Daniel pretended to be reading a book. Lying on his back, he held it to the sky, and found its pages framed in blue. He was thinking how like a bird a book could be, how brooding, self-contained and secret.

Suddenly he felt the book lift from his hand. The pages flapped in the wind as if they were straining

sunwards, and all the words poured down on him like
lark song.

'Where do they get their ideas from?'

Someone's finger was braced against the spine.
Looking up Daniel saw Timon standing just behind
him. Branches sprouted from his head, and his hands
were rough as bark. Daniel had the fleeting impression
of some kind of mossy growth on his clothes and skin.
The world span as Daniel rolled himself upright.
Timon held the book out, nipped with distaste between
forefinger and thumb.

'A bit old for this?'

'Perhaps. I'm catching up on my reading. I missed
out when I was the right age, remember?'

'How would I know?' said Timon dismissively. 'I
wasn't around.'

'No.' Daniel took back the book.

'Touché,' smiled Timon. 'I haven't been much of a
big brother, have I?'

'Forget it,' said Daniel.

'I can't forget. That's why I'm going to make it up to
you.'

'Make it up? How?' asked Daniel, and saw the edge
of Timon's mouth quiver with the consciousness of
having said too much. 'Just how are you going to make
it up to me?'

'That would be telling, wouldn't it? I'm sure I don't
need to, with your lively mind.'

Daniel was having trouble following Timon's words.
Whenever he looked straight at him, his brother's face
was turned in his direction, candid and ironic in quick
succession. But beyond that, at the edge of his vision,
he had a sense of turmoil. There, Timon was hardly
different from the twigs and greenery around him. As

Timon paced about him in a figure of eight, Daniel seemed at times to be talking to the wood itself, at times to the air.

'Sit down, Timon. Come into the hide. Do you want some tea?'

'Thanks, I need a drink. You have a stove in there? I'm impressed.' Timon poked his head into the hide, and withdrew it hastily. 'A bit stuffy for me, though. I've become an outdoor sort of person. A stepchild of the elements these six years.'

'I'll take that as a yes.'

Daniel lit the Primus. It gave him a chance to think, and to guess at Timon's new business with him. He had been wrong too often, his capacity for certainty was shot. One thing was for sure, Timon was not a stranger posing as his brother. He knew too much for that. Not just facts, but all the secret contours of their life together – things that escaped words and could not have been confided. But he was not his brother either, not as Daniel had known him. Too many things were wrong. He had been brewed up from the right ingredients, but all the proportions were out. Bubbles clung to the sides of the saucepan as it heated, then bobbed and burst over the quickening surface.

They sat down, and Timon took the mug.

'So what's her back yard like?' asked Daniel.

'Come again?'

'Jane Garfield's back yard. You've been creeping round there, haven't you?'

'You've lost me, squire,' said Timon, turning cockney. But he didn't seem surprised enough, and Daniel thought his guess had been right.

'It doesn't matter. So long as we understand each other.'

Timon seemed to accept that. He looked at the writing on the mug. If Timon were not immune to embarrassment, Daniel would have suspected him. He took courage from that. And Daniel needed courage, to say what he had to say now.

'Actually, you've always been around, haven't you?'

'Pardon?'

'You were here the whole time, watching. And then, after six years, out of the shadows you came. What gave you the final nudge?'

Timon sat crossed-legged on the ground. The mug was forgotten, and he span a stick between his hands as if he were making fire.

Daniel said: 'You are dead, aren't you? That was just a story, about living on the street.'

His brother leant forward till his face almost kissed the earth. He sat like that for a long time.

'You are a ghost, aren't you?' repeated Daniel.

He noticed that Timon's head was trembling. The movement was slight, but gradually it grew till his whole body from the waist up shook with laughter. 'Well done, little brother! You've worked me out! I haven't been scrabbling a living with the crusties, I've been down among the dead men. What tipped you off?'

'Don't laugh at me.'

'I'd expect this from a certain aged aunt, not you. Death before dishonour, is it? Better I should meet a watery fate than ... what's the word? Besmirch, I think – besmirch the family name through beggary. A name that never was besmirched before, as you well know.'

But Timon's smile, when he lifted his face, was dangerous.

'Glasgow, I was, the first two years. I had to find a

—— 114 ——

place where no one knew me, but big enough to hide. London was too obvious. Every ragged runaway heads there. But in Scotland I felt at home. Ever lain yourself down on Sauchiehall Street on a Saturday night? What a buzz! The things I've seen ...'

'You never went away, Timon. You stayed, and you turned this place into hell. You worked at it.'

'Look, I know what I put you through. I lost count of the times I was on the point of getting in touch. The unposted cards I've dropped into Glasgow's handsome municipal bins! But I couldn't do it, don't you see?'

'I don't see anything.'

'Not just for my sake, for yours. It would only have put you in danger if you'd known where I was. At least if you thought I was dead you could put me behind you, build a new life. I didn't want to get in the way of that.'

'This is sweet.'

'You don't believe me?' said Timon, hurt.

'We're not strangers. No, I don't believe you ever could change. I don't believe you went to Glasgow. This whole thing has been a blind – and you blinded me for a while. But the truth is different. You stayed, in the house, in my head. You didn't have the nerve to leave, probably. Could be something nasty was waiting for you – I don't know. Is there such a place as hell?'

Timon glanced at him sharply. His hands whitened with the pressure of holding his mug. 'You said this place was hell. And frankly, to judge by your tea—'

'When you're dead, where do you go? I can't see you with a harp, Timon. How about the other place? Those creeps on the dock – what did you mean when you said you were a runaway? Who were you running from?'

'Shut up about them! I've told you, anyway.'

—— 115 ——

'They weren't criminals. It wasn't them who left you on the sand that night. They weren't even flesh and blood.' Daniel forced himself to look Timon in the face. 'And nor are you.'

'What are you saying? Are you expecting me to walk through a wall? Look!' Timon dropped the mug. A glossy tongue of brown liquid licked the earth and was swallowed. 'Could a ghost break your souvenir from St Ives?' he asked, poking at the pieces with his toe.

'I don't know. I'm not an expert. Maybe it could do all kinds of things.'

'Then you need another kind of proof. Take my hand. No? Then follow me.' Timon got to his feet, with a tinkle from the baubles hanging about his neck. He did not look back, but led Daniel down the short, steep slope of creepers and gorse to Morton's Pond. The fence at this point was hanging like a curtain, which Timon drew back to pass. 'It's all right,' he said, noticing Daniel hesitate. 'I'm not about to push you under.'

'Then what's the idea?'

'I want to show you something. Ghosts have no reflection, right?' Using a stick he skimmed the green scum from the water at his feet. 'Check me out.'

'I thought that was vampires. The reflection thing.'

'Too much Hollywood, Daniel. Too much popcorn in your brain. Come on – you have nothing to lose but your lunch.'

Daniel inched down the slope, and grabbed hold of a bush.

In the water the trees played at cat's cradle.

Daniel saw his own face, and beside him a tall, lean figure. The reflection merged with something that was below the water's surface, a coil of tiny worms writhing for the shade. They punctured Timon's skin. Timon's bleached face hung like a mask from high branches. His body was vapour.

'What do you see?'

'I don't see my brother.'

There was a rush of air above him, as if a balloon were being let down. 'That's a pity,' sighed Timon's voice, which was in the rush of air so that he too seemed to be leaking away. Then he added with a mischievous nostalgia: 'Just one push, Daniel. Just one little push.'

Daniel felt his feet begin to slip from beneath him. He was sliding down to the water, over the crumbling earth, the catches of twig and root. The old panic rose as his breath left him. His face scraped the soil, before his fingers found a hold on a jutting stone. He looked back up the slope, but Timon was already gone. His feet were damp, and his breath short from the poisoned air.

'You should have more trust in people, Daniel!' It was Timon's voice. From the hide, at first – and then from the darkest spinney, and everywhere. A foot stamping on the ground above sent a little avalanche of stones and earth. Daniel hauled himself up to the fence, and caught sight of Timon's back, as a tangle of rags lacing itself out between branches.

Daniel stood and swiped the clinging ivy from his legs, and most of the dirt. He could feel his pulse beat madly, and nausea from breathing poison. Almost at once he had to sit down again. He sat there until he was sure that he was alone, and could move his head without pain. Gradually he began to notice things: the way the shadows bobbed on the pond's surface, the platoon of ants scouting his trouser leg. Hearing birdsong above him, he realised that he had come to a conclusion, without knowing quite how: a little nugget of certainty concerning Timon.

He realised too he was crying: crying because Timon was dead. Timon was lost, and everything that had happened over the last weeks had been a dream, a dream with an awakening at the end of it. A chill entered his bones as he thought of the sea's dead in all their thousands: the dead that sailed the salt foam from ocean to shore, blown with the night mist, the gull's wing. The fog-horn carried them, and the distant swell, and in they came with every tide, haunting the sea ports. They waited, implacable. Once, people made names for them and warned their children: 'Watch out for Peg Powler, Jenny Greenteeth! Don't stray too near the water's cdge!'

But on certain nights the cattle were driven into shelter, the doors barred.

For sometimes they left the water.

Eleven

THERE WAS NOWHERE TO GO BUT MARLEY'S, and right now that was the best place. Mrs Kinsale asked no questions, and nor did Mary, Diane or Elaine. Daniel knew that whatever happened to him, Marley's would still keep the same Marley smell, of beeswax and bergamot. The cherry shortbread would still shiver into pieces at the sight of a knife blade. At three the Delillo sisters would order cakes, and at three-forty precisely they would look at their watches, scold themselves and leave. Lunch was a sandwich and an apple, and something from the cake trolley that Mrs Kinsale would slip him every day as if it were an unheard-of indulgence.

At ten to five Daniel was making an attempt on the washing up, when he had an unexpected visitor.

'I saw Janie last night.'

Meg Aitken's voice. Daniel turned, to see her settling her face into a pair of smugly-cupped hands. Framed by the serving hatch she was trying to look mysterious, but Meg was no Mona Lisa.

'I saw—'

'I heard! I'm busy, can't you see?' He sluiced a soup bowl under the cold tap. What was Meg doing in Marley's anyway?

'It's almost five o'clock. Always gets quiet around now. I thought you might fancy a chat.'

'No thanks.'

'A shoulder to cry on?'

Daniel stiffened. 'I'd rather not.'

Meg smiled faintly. 'Know how to charm a girl, don't you? Real way with words. Have to admit it.' She was in the back room, somehow, beside him. 'I'm a bit smitten with you myself.'

'Yes?'

'I can't help it.' She began fiddling with his apron strings.

'Go away, Meg.'

'Suit yourself.' Her hands were raised at once in wide-eyed surrender. 'I was only trying to be friendly.'

For thirty seconds he busied himself stacking cups.

'She was with Gabriel.'

'Who was?' Daniel said, acting as dumb as he felt.

'Giggling away in the movie queue. The new Tom Cruise, it was. They looked very friendly.'

Cutlery rattled through Daniel's hands. Plates. Cups. He filled the sink with fresh water.

'Snuggling up together.'

'It's cold these nights.'

'Gabriel's a real angel, lending her his jacket. Specially while he's still wearing it.'

'Are you finished yet?' He tossed a fistful of suds in her direction. 'Just listen. What Jane does is her business. We're not together. We never were together. That's it – *comprendez*?' He felt better for being delivered of this lie. No point in wasting the truth of it on Meg. No point in letting her revel in all that.

Not that she'd believe him, anyway. Jane was her

best friend, after all. Of course she knew the whole story.

'She was too old for you,' Meg began again. 'You know that?'

'She won't be seventeen till next month.'

'There are different ways of being older, love. Just because you've lived more days doesn't mean you know the first thing about—'

'Don't "love" me!'

'—*l'amour*. And how can I help loving you? When you're so …'

'Meg, get off! Mrs Kinsale's out in the cold store.'

'So? She's probably deaf as a post. Come on, relax for once in your life!'

Daniel stepped back, straight into the rack of wine glasses. A dozen smashed in a crystal hail at his feet. The noise was awful.

Meg stared.

Then came Mrs Kinsale's voice, returning from the cold store. 'Daniel! Daniel! Goodness, have you hurt yourself?'

Max was at sea. For the last ten minutes Mrs Kinsale had been talking to him on the phone, alternately apologising and accusing Daniel of some offence involving glasses, cake and at least one girl.

'I'm not a complaining woman, Mr Hilliard. And heaven knows, I'm not a prude.'

'Of course not,' soothed Max. He glanced despairingly at the television, where a complicated murder plot was about to be unravelled. Would his suspicion of the wheelchair-bound breeder of racehorses be vindicated? He had been in Marley's only once, but his memory was of a sedate and intensely respectable establishment

– a place where the pastries were arranged in tiers. Mrs Kinsale's story did not fit this picture at all.

'The people who come to Marley's, it's peace and quiet they're looking for. Something like this does us no good.'

'I do understand. If you'll just tot up the damage, you can send me the bill—'

'But more than anything else it's a matter of trust. I need to feel I can get on with things without having to check up every two minutes. You run a business yourself, so you'll know what I mean.'

Max immediately thought of his new partner, Titia. Had she tried to steal his thunder over the contract with the Exhibition Centre? The thought drew a thousand daytime worries after it: appointments to make and break, bargains to be driven, suppliers to chase. Meanwhile he was assuring Mrs Kinsale that he knew exactly what she meant. He couldn't think what had got into Daniel.

'I can only imagine that he tripped backwards over something,' he added with sudden invention. 'Are there any jutting-out cupboards in your kitchen? Perhaps he caught his ankle?'

'There are no jutting cupboards at Marley's,' Mrs Kinsale told him crisply. 'I know what you're trying to do, Mr Hilliard. You're trying to protect Daniel by turning the blame back onto me. Well, I run a safe kitchen. It is not equipped for teenage Romeos, but in all other respects it is perfectly suited to its function.'

'I can see you've made up your mind,' Max conceded.

'It's not with any pleasure, you understand.'

'I do. I do.'

Max put down the receiver, and gave a little whistle

of wonder at the turn of events. So Daniel had been sacked because of some girl! A pity. Indeed, a pity. But there were other jobs – he had noticed several vacancies on his last visit to Tesco. And at least it was a girl behind it! Max knew that Lisa had been worried about that side of things. He wished he'd had the presence of mind to ask her name. But it sounded rather a hectic episode, not unlike several in Max's own career. Yes, the more he thought about it, the better omen it seemed, and the more so because on television the detective was still busy arranging his suspects in the library. Max leaned back in Aunt Jenkins' vacant armchair, turned the volume up, and waited for justice to be dispensed.

Daniel had not wanted to talk to anyone. It was not the loss of the job at Marley's, nor even the way Meg had laughed about it afterwards. It was the look on Mrs Kinsale's face. She had been disappointed in him – hurt. He realised only now that her good opinion mattered. Mrs Kinsale, silly and affected, who taped frilly bits of paper round her cakes, had cared what happened to him. Come to that, he hardly knew her – never thought about her from one Marley's session to the next. But she had trusted him, enough to be hurt.

He sat by the black stone fort on the headland, where they had once kept prisoners – was it in Napoleon's time? The lights on the incoming tide were a shoal of lanterns, lanterns darting to and fro where the brisk wind met the current. *They'll all come now.* The ghost tide was running in, fringed with foam, lurching the sea against breakwaters. He had thought Timon might find him here, but Timon for once had not shown himself. The fort stuck sharp nodules of flint into his spine. In the last hour Daniel had watched the day fail, the sun drop into the sea like a dishcloth, without a spark of red. The twilight seemed endless, grey; yet at last the lighthouse down the coast had begun its watch, and the floating restaurant in the harbour lit its fairy lights. He lifted himself and made his way downhill, to the place where the tarmac path ran into bollards and a small car park. Beyond, the sea wall hugged the windy boulevard. The fort behind him sat on a grey horizon. A coastguard chopper drummed along its battlements.

It was as he left the car park that he became aware of his brother's presence. Dressed in black, Timon was huddled on the sheltered side of the wooden kiosk where they took the motorists' money.

'Daniel!' He came forward, awkward. 'Daniel?'

'Yes?' said Daniel. He was suddenly conscious of the dark, and the loneliness of the place.

'About earlier … at the pond. I was angry. I'm sorry.'

'*You* were angry?'

Timon raised his hand, acknowledging the injustice of it. He walked with him a few steps, then stopped abruptly. 'Do you trust me, Daniel?'

'What have you done to make me trust you?' retorted Daniel.

'Nothing yet, I know that. But I will, Daniel. Before this night is out, I'll give you a reason to thank me. You'll see what I can do.'

'There's no need—' Daniel began in alarm.

'But there is!' replied Timon. 'I'm scared, you see. Scared I'll become one of *them*, forget how to be human. It happens. It was happening to me even before—'

Timon stopped short, with a cough cracking his

lungs like bladderwrack. He crouched, suddenly small inside his greatcoat.

'Before you drowned,' said Daniel.

Timon's eyes sparkled, but he seemed in a daze, and did not deny it. Still coughing, he brought up a mouthful of froth onto his sleeve, white with darker flecks. 'Have you seen the moon?' he asked.

Daniel glanced at the moon, just risen and still ghostly. 'What about it?'

'It's almost full again. I'll do well to last the month, I think. There were a dozen of us at first, thrown up by the storm: I may be the only one left. But now the sea will be pulling its strongest, pulling the flesh from my bones, the breath from my body. I'm going, you see? I can't delay it, the planet won't stop for me.'

Daniel looked at him uncomprehendingly. 'But how did you come back at all? If you were … gone?'

'Let's say I was beached, say the high tide dropped me. When the storms come, things get disturbed. Sea, land, life and death – those words don't mean so much. Chance put me here, a crazy thing, living and drowned. It's all chance. Oh, and when I awoke, I thought – yes, a chance to get it right this time. All the stupid things I did. They come back to haunt you – you don't sleep easy with those dreams. Only there's not much time.'

The sea sucked its teeth.

'You don't need to do anything for me,' said Daniel. 'I'm all right.'

'Is that so? I saw what happened this afternoon. How you let yourself get walked over by that girl.'

'What did you see?' Daniel asked doubtfully.

'Shops have doors, and customers have ears. You

didn't notice me, that's all. Face it, Daniel, you *need* a big brother.'

'I'm all right!' repeated Daniel.

'Yeah, sure! "Take your hands off, Meg!"' Timon squeaked out a falsetto.

'I can handle it, Timon! It's none of your business!'

Timon gave a quick smile then, to show the mockery was in fun. But a moment later he leant over and took Daniel by the throat, hissing: 'You owe me! It was because of you I ended up this way. If anyone should have been left down there on the sand, it was you. But I haven't made you pay, Daniel. I've been generous. Just don't think you can fob me off now.'

Daniel felt Timon's salt breath touch him. For the first time he understood how *alien* was this creature, who had once been his brother. And he was afraid.

'I didn't force you to get involved with criminals,' he whispered with a dry tongue. 'You did that for yourself.'

'Yeah. I forgot, you're perfect. The perfect boy in his perfect family. And soon you'll have a perfect little sister too.'

Daniel hesitated. 'What's that to you?'

Timon gave a secret smile. 'No one likes to be left behind entirely. I know you're all trying your best to forget me – but maybe I won't allow it.'

'Is that a threat?' asked Daniel.

'Did it sound like one? I apologise.' Timon collapsed back against the wall of the kiosk, but with one hand out to grab the railing that ran alongside it. He said, quiet again: 'I need a boost, Daniel. I can't outrun them, not for ever, not without nourishment. Without food, how can I sustain myself? How can I keep up appearances?'

As he spoke, the hand that gripped the railing seemed to change, and through the raindrops now dotting Timon's skin Daniel saw that the word LESS had faded – that in fact the skin itself had somehow thinned, become translucent. The muscles and tendons knitting the bones of his hand were visible. The blood's pumping fattened the black veins. At his wrist a mess of split and bruised vessels showed where he had once struggled – perhaps for his life, perhaps losing. The vision held Daniel in horrible fascination, a spell he knew he had to break or go mad. As he wrenched his gaze away the sight righted itself. The skin thickened again: and Timon's face, when Daniel dared look at it, was the same elegant oval, with the same cunning eyes, and the teeth that were yellow, and the gaps where teeth should be.

'They won't give up,' said Timon at last. Daniel knew he meant the Lockermen. 'The laws they enforce – they're the laws of nature.'

'I'm sorry,' stammered Daniel. 'I'm sorry, I've got to go.' He could stay no longer: his courage had deserted him.

He was moving down to the road, when Timon called him back: 'Oh Daniel!'

'Yes?' Daniel returned, warily.

'Have you got any change? I may need to pay a fare soon.'

Daniel felt in his pocket, and found his last fiver. It left his hand for Timon's, fluttered in an instant cage of fingers, and was gone.

'You watch!' Timon called as Daniel turned away again. 'Soon! You'll see what I can do!'

Daniel set off at a fast pace, and did not look back. The city drew him in with tentacles of light.

Distances shrank, dwindling the horizon to the paving stone before his foot. A restaurant-scented breeze blew the surf from him, made him a street creature once again. The people he passed talked to each other, or kept their eyes averted, and let him dredge the gutter with his toe. For an hour he walked, till at length he found himself near the bus station, no more than an underpass away. He looked at his watch and wondered if he should go home: it was just nine-thirty.

From the entrance of the underpass he heard a harmonica playing the blues. He paused; then continued down the steps.

The neon strip lights flickered in the stairwell. When Daniel tried, he could make it seem as if they were synchronised with the mouth organ. If the Harmonica Man trilled on a high note, the lights followed his lead. If he sank into silence, the lights plunged Daniel in darkness up to his waist, just the reflection of the ground-level shop windows glimmering on his torso. With an electric clunk the strips of brightness sprang back to life; but this time the silence remained. The Harmonica Man was packing up for the night.

Daniel rounded the corner and saw him. The Harmonica Man looked smaller now, as he picked up the hat where he'd been collecting coins and funnelled them into his jacket pocket. The jacket sagged with the weight. He stood, and put the hat on his head, still humming a blues melody. It must have been a good day.

'You, in the corner there!' he cried suddenly. He turned to Daniel. 'Are you coming any closer? Or do I have to shout?'

Daniel came forward hesitantly. 'Can I talk to you?'

'Later. Don't you know this place is dangerous at

night?' The Harmonica Man laughed, and waited at the foot of the steps. Daniel, who had been afraid the Harmonica Man might think he was a mugger, nevertheless felt a little hurt at being considered so obviously harmless. But he followed him obediently.

The Harmonica Man's place was close by, up some steps in Kingston Street. A pair of black bins blocked his door, and the windows were boarded up: in daylight Daniel would probably have thought it derelict. The Harmonica Man took out some keys – three heavy mortices and a Yale lock – and let them in, waiting till the door was shut before reaching for the light. They were in a small, bare-plastered hallway. To the left was a kitchenette, to the right a bed-sitting room, with one armchair and a foldaway table beside it. Daniel followed, but was forced to stop as the Harmonica Man abruptly turned just beyond the doorway.

'I've been wondering if you'd come,' he said, looking at him intently. 'Ever since the other day, at the roundabout – I saw you staring at me. You have a look of Timon.'

'I've got some things need straightening out. Questions.'

'What else? Come in, then. You can make a space in that chair. Never mind the cat.'

Daniel picked his way forward. He felt reluctant to close the door behind him: partly because it offered a means of escape, but also because the air in the Harmonica Man's flat was unbreathable. The cat would not move, and he squeezed in between it and the chair's high wooden arm.

'You knew my brother then?' said Daniel.

'I knew him slightly,' said the Harmonica Man,

seating himself on the bed. He spoke in precise terms, as if he were on oath. 'He had a reputation. Gin?'

The Harmonica Man was suddenly on his feet, and making towards a food safe in which a bottle of gin chinked against a solitary glass. 'You take the glass, I'll have mine in the mug. Guests are guests.'

'No, thanks.'

'Aw, you're not going to drink my gin?' chided the Harmonica Man, still smiles.

'I don't like gin,' Daniel began – then saw the Harmonica Man's expression change to offence and anger. He felt that he had failed a test. 'Just a glass then,' he said quickly. 'To keep you company.'

'That's my man!' chuckled the Harmonica Man, but largely to himself. 'Call me Adler,' he added, lighting a cigarette.

Daniel sipped at the gin. 'I'm glad I found you tonight. I need you to tell me what happened to Timon.'

Adler raised one sceptical eyebrow. 'What could I know about that? I'm just the attendant at the toilets in the underpass. I scrub out the pans, keep the walls clean. You must have been given bad information.'

His hand curled itself about his mug, and he shrank himself into the part: a sad old man, not worth talking to. But Daniel remembered the way he had seen off the drunk, Fuller. There had been nothing negligible about him then. His voice had carried authority: Fuller had skulked off like a chastened dog. In his own world the Harmonica Man was important.

'But you knew Timon – you said that yourself.'

'Sure, I knew him, like everyone knew him. He got around. I liked him, too. He had a fire – you understand? Something inside.'

'You knew about the drugs?'

Adler paused, and swirled the liquid in his mug pensively.

'Timon had a lot of friends, I guess – friends in low places. It doesn't matter now.'

Adler smiled charmingly.

'What happened, then? How did he die?'

'He did an Alka Seltzer, didn't he? Plink plink fizz – splash in the harbour. Fell off the harbour wall, that's what I heard. Someone dared him.'

'That's not what they said at the inquest.'

Adler raised a hand. 'I'm telling you like they told me. You know something different, fine. Why you asking me then?'

'The inquest said he was murdered.'

The man grinned slowly. 'Murder Timon? Now who would want to do that?' The pink tongue lolled just inside his lip, ready to ring out a peal of mockery.

'Dealers. If they thought he'd cheated them, they might want to kill him.'

Adler's dark glasses had two hissing yellow flames in their centres where he watched the flicker of his cigarette lighter. Adler was a dealer, for sure. He might have his reasons, in a world where liking didn't count for much, to want Timon dead.

'Who would put themselves to that kind of trouble? Killing's risky, it draws attention. Timon was just a kid. He was no threat to anyone.'

'Maybe he knew too much.'

'Timon knew nothing. You think Timon was knocking on some big-time doors? Just look around you. This is Timon's world.'

Tins lay half empty, with mould growing. The bed was a stinking mattress. From garage calendars naked women smiled down; between, the walls were streaked with dirt. If money ever came here, it did not stay.

'Here, drink up. You look sad.' Adler poured another inch of gin into the glass. Daniel's temples throbbed, and his words fumbled their way forward.

'Your boss. There must be a whole chain. You can tell me …' Adler was looking blurry, leaning back and forth. 'Names and things.'

'Forget it, son, forget it. There are things you cannot touch in this world. You cannot touch the sky. And there are people you cannot touch. So forget it. If you can find your way home tonight, say a prayer and know that you are lucky. That's all.'

'But I need to know—'

'Look, you want some bigshot reason for your brother getting killed? There wasn't any. Nothing led to it, nothing led from it. Just a mess – a waste, like most things.'

Daniel was trying to remember what he had heard, and when. Lisa had tried to shield him from everything to do with Timon's death. She had kept the TV remote in arm's reach when the local news came on. She had cancelled the papers, or bought and read them when Daniel was at school. Even now there were things she would never speak of, questions he had trained himself not to ask. But in the playground, on the street, her careful indoor silences were blown away. What did it matter how he knew? Plastic straps had bound Timon's wrists, and at the other end were looped through the poles that had staked him to the sand bank, near the shifting tidal waters, the cruisers and the wide boats. There his brother had drowned.

'Are you all right, kid?'

'Yes, I'm fine, Mr Adler.'

But Daniel's pursuit of memory had led him to stare too hard at the cracked plaster of Adler's ceiling, and then at the dingy-psychedelic curtains, where two swirls of colour had turned themselves into a pair of eyes, which were owl's eyes, and dangerous.

'But Timon didn't fall off the harbour wall,' he said. 'You know that.'

'Listen,' said Adler softly, 'there were all kinds of rumours. Why bother with details? When someone's dead, what else do you need to know? There's just a fact, a wall you can knock your head against, or walk away from. Save yourself the bruises, son. Be happy.'

Daniel grinned, but he could feel his smile a death's-head. 'I'm very happy, can't you tell?' He fingered the edge of his knuckle, inlaid with a frond of blood where he had scraped the wall of the fort. 'I'll go now. I'm fine.'

Abruptly Adler leaned forward, and said in a quick, low voice: 'Your brother made promises he couldn't keep. More than once, and to the wrong people. He was a go-between – you understand me? He took money for goods he didn't deliver, made fools out of them. Bad move.'

'Out of you too?' Daniel dared to reply. 'Timon was meant to give you a packet. He's dead because of it. How come you got through all right?'

'Ha!' scoffed Adler. 'Did I get through all right?'

He laid his hand upon the arm of the chair where Daniel sat. It was a beautiful hand, with ebony skin, with delicate strong fingers. A subtle hand, versatile and cunning. Except that two of the fingers were missing, cut off below the first knuckle.

'They used bolt-cutters,' said Adler. 'There wasn't any anaesthetic, but that didn't matter – I wasn't conscious for long.' He grinned at Daniel's stupefied face, and leant down to whisper in his ear again: 'Go home! Take some good advice for once!'

This time though it was not advice, it was a dismissal. Daniel raised himself to his feet, dizzy for a moment as he stood.

As he touched the handle of the door, Daniel saw the local paper on the rug. '*MP calls for firm measures on homeless.*' An angry man stared from the inset picture: 'Hose them from the shop doors!' Adler was not homeless: he had this place, a hole in the wall to call his own. But he knew the homeless. The drunks in that sunken well of a roundabout were his companions. A few pounds a week separated him from them. What they knew and saw, he knew and saw also.

'Have you heard of the Lockermen?' asked Daniel, on impulse.

'The *what*?'

'They may be called other things too. The Night Watch.'

'And who are these people? Friends of yours?'

'No! They're nobody's friends. They're not human at all, I think. They come from the sea … They take children. I saw.'

Adler moved behind him to the door. 'Go home and get some rest, son,' he said, gripping the door's edge with two fingers and a thumb. 'Listen, I've tried to help you out, because you look like you need it. But don't take advantage, eh? Know when to stop.'

Daniel left the house. As he squeezed between the bins back onto Kingston Street he heard the sound of the mortice locks being turned behind him. No light showed from between the curtains. He retraced his steps to the underpass, down Hills Road and some sharp concrete steps where the sign pointed out the bus station. The gin had left him dazed and fearless. He marvelled at how little the Harmonica Man had told him, and how certain his sense of Timon had nevertheless become. It was strange, to be getting to know his brother only now, six years too late. By now even Timon's ghost was thin and waning. But the will behind it was the same, and Daniel could not guess what it would do. Tomorrow he would figure it out.

But tonight was not yet over. As he passed the bend in the underpass he felt a hand grab his collar, and twist it like a garrotte. He sensed someone at his back, and others. Hands were seizing his legs and arms. He was conscious of sniggers behind him. A memory of the Lockermen flashed into his mind and turned his fearlessness of a moment before to water. A wet mouth was put close against his ear.

'I've seen the way you've been eyeing up Jane Garfield,' hissed Gabriel Spicer.

Daniel gasped with relief. Beside everything else the threat of Gabriel Spicer seemed laughable. He hardly took in what he was saying.

'She's not for you, toe-rag,' said Gabriel. 'You know what? You're sad. I'm telling you what she says. A loser. She laughs at you.'

That was a lie. Daniel was thinking of smart things to say, but the smart thing was to say nothing. He knew that.

'You're a liar,' he replied.

The garrotte tightened. 'You don't get it, do you? I'm telling you nicely, because I've got a kind heart.' One of Gabriel's friends sniggered. 'I don't like to see you get hurt, understand?'

Daniel examined the bricks in the wall beside his

head. English Bond, English Bond, the good old English Bond.

'*Understand*?'

'Very sorry, the English she is not so good.'

He was being jostled against the wall. He was bent double, the wind knocked from his stomach. Four faces leered at him. Gabriel and two friends, and the third-year Lacey who ran his errands. Lacey's smile was broadest, and he kept hopping about as if he needed a bush to pee behind.

'We could have you now,' said one of Gabriel's friends.

Gabriel's foot flashed out, and caught Daniel on the shin. He felt himself falling, clutching at the ground. His eyes filled. More kicks came raining in, on the ribs, the hands, the mouth. Daniel realised that they were hurting, but the pain was some way off. In fact the sensation of distance was growing. It grew until he could hardly see or hear his attackers, still less defend himself.

Finally there was nothing he could see or hear.

Twelve

DANIEL'S LIP HAD COME OFF WORST. THE FLOW of blood onto his tongue showed no sign of stopping. When he laid one finger gently on the place he knew why: there was a groove where the top of his smile ought to be. He took his finger off again, a little squeamish, and blinked. One eye closed more easily than the other, but he could still see out of both. He touched his arm tenderly. Joints and fingers worked as his brain told them. Then he slumped back, exhausted.

There were footsteps coming towards him, along the underpass. One of *them*, back for more. No: he could hear the shoes click from this far off – it was a woman. He did not look up. The footsteps slowed hesitantly as they turned the corner, then hastened to get past.

'Shcuse me.' His voice sounded thick and slurred. It was hard to talk with this lip. He heard himself asking for help. He sounded drunk.

The footsteps hurried on, trailing scent. Daniel saw a bag, black tights, blue regulation skirt – and realised it must be a nurse. A nurse had walked right past him! He tried to shout after her, but couldn't; then he didn't want to. Couldn't blame her. Couldn't blame anyone but himself. *Tip tap* went the shoes up the steps to the bus station, and disappeared.

He was cold.

He woke a while later, to find his legs covered with a tartan blanket. He sat up with a start, and looked about him. The underpass was deserted. Someone had tucked a coin into his hand, and wiped his mouth – his handkerchief lay a few feet away. The blood on it was his own, he supposed.

At last he tried to stand. He pushed himself against the wall, and squirmed his shoulders up caterpillar style, but quickly had to slump back. The pain in his ribs was bad: he tried to keep his breathing shallow. He glanced at his watch. It was gone, of course. His wrist was red and sore where they had pulled the strap. He remembered that now, how they pulled and pulled, before one of them finally thought to undo the buckle. Stupid, all of them. Daniel checked his pockets. He'd had no money to lose, and the keys were no use to them. They were so stupid.

Then why was he the one lying in the underpass, spitting blood?

By the time he returned to Morton's Holt it was two o'clock, and a light rain was stabbing at his face and hands. He had walked the five miles from the city centre. The buses had shut down for the night. Once he had tried to hail a taxi, and almost stumbled into the gutter as it passed him. Not having the money, he had hoped to cadge the fare from Max or Lisa when he got home: then thought it best to walk.

The walk had steadied him too, as the gin worked through his system, and he sang, and limpingly skipped, and burped up juniper, and failed to recognise it among the early blossoms of the nearby gardens. A full moon watched him go – a full, tide-tugging moon – before the clouds closed in on it and rained.

The lights were on inside the house. Only Aunt

Jenkins' window was blank, and Ruby's, who was staying the night in town. Daniel was blearily surprised at this, and surprised at the sight of Max's Rover still ungaraged – Max who was normally diligent in such things. It then occurred to him, as it had not since he awoke in the underpass, that they would be seriously worried by his absence. He squatted beside Max's wing mirror, exploring by the porch light the state of his face, and manufacturing explanations for it. Something approximately true seemed best, and he pieced together the tale of a random mugger, whose own face he had not seen, and who had left him in a shop's backyard. Climbing out had cost him a split lip, and a tumble into dustbins. Gabriel Spicer's name did not appear.

He let himself in through the unlocked back door, to find the kitchen empty. A string quartet was playing in the living-room, and he crossed the hall to find it, flexing his sluggish tongue to tell the story he had prepared. On the sofa Max and Lisa were sitting together. Lisa's hands were plunged into the pockets of a baggy cardigan. Daniel could tell that he was in at the end of a long evening. A lot of words had already been said. His mother had been crying.

'Hello, Mum, Max,' he said.

There was silence. All at once Lisa was on her feet and hugging him. 'You're all right,' she was murmuring, as if it astonished her. 'Thank God.'

'I'm fine, Mum. I'm sorry I didn't let you know. I couldn't get to a phone.' Daniel lied badly. The fine details of his story were already lost, as he stumbled forward into the shocking fact that his mother was crying on his shoulder. 'You didn't have to wait up.'

'But where have you been? And what's happened to your face?'

'That's something we'd all like to know,' added Max, who had not left the sofa, but rather sunk down deeper. He seemed to be settling in for a siege.

'Can we talk about it in the morning? I'm tired. You too, I'm sure. Let's have some Ovaltine and bed.'

'Not so tired that we can't listen while you say how you came by those injuries,' rejoined Max. 'Has anyone had a look at them? A doctor?'

'There's no need, Max, really. They look worse than they are.'

'We should see the other fellow, huh?' said Max drily. 'Why not tell us all about it?'

Daniel opened his mouth to begin the explanation he'd prepared. But something in Lisa's look warned him not to try. 'I'd rather wait, till the morning anyway.'

'Let him sleep, Max – we've all had a very long evening,' said Lisa.

'Rather more than that, I'd say,' said Max, standing. 'It's not every day I find myself accused of being related to a vandal and a street brawler. Do you think I'm going to let that pass?' A black ink-jet of anger had suddenly stained his voice.

Daniel blinked at him. 'Who's accusing you of anything?'

'Martin Spicer, for the moment. Tomorrow, probably the police. So if you don't mind I'll pass up the bedtime drink and ask you what you meant by putting Gabriel Spicer in hospital.'

'*Hospital?*'

'And don't play the innocent, or I'll be ringing the

police myself. You've really overstepped the mark this time, Daniel.'

'Are you saying that Gabriel's hurt?'

'A broken nose, rib fractures, possible concussion – yes, he's hurt. Not that you hung around to find out.'

'I don't know anything about it,' Daniel began, but a gesture from his mother cut him off.

'Daniel – don't drag yourself in deeper. You were seen.'

'I don't know what you're talking about!'

'Don't!' she pleaded, looking down at the floor.

'Mum, read my lips. *I … never … touched … Gabriel!*'

'Your lip says different,' Max observed. 'And so do Tommy Lacey, and the rest. But let me refresh your memory. Marley's – remember? You thought it would be fun to lob a couple of bricks through the window, to get back at Mrs Kinsale for firing you. Glass splinters in the tea cakes, all that mess in her little starch kingdom. A satisfying revenge, no doubt. Except that you let yourself be seen – and by people who knew you too. I'll leave you to fill in the differences that followed with Gabriel Spicer and his friends – I'm not particularly interested in details. It's enough that you used the second brick on Gabriel.'

'This is fantasy.'

'Then how do you explain your own condition? Look at yourself!'

Daniel caught sight of his reflection in the mirror hanging above the mantelpiece. He looked like an illustration to Max's sermon, with his lip split and swollen, and bloodstains flowering on his shirt.

'What does Gabriel say?' he asked. 'Does he say I attacked him?'

'Gabriel's been in no fit state to talk. But that little

— 141 —

friend of his, the Lacey lad, he saw you clearly enough. He was frightened out of his wits, according to Martin Spicer.'

'Gabriel's father's been round here this evening,' Lisa explained. 'He wasn't very happy, to say the least.'

'The man's a lunatic,' added Max. 'Poking me in the chest as if *I* was to blame! But it's not surprising he's angry …'

'OK,' said Daniel, 'you want the truth? I never attacked Gabriel – it was the other way round. Him and his friends did this to me – I never got the chance to hit back. And it was in the underpass at the shopping centre. I haven't been near Marley's since it closed.'

Max's face was a mask of disbelief.

'You think I could have taken them all on and won? Have you seen the size of Gabriel Spicer? This is me, Daniel – not the Karate Kid.'

'If there were two sides to it that's something we can go into later. But one thing you can't deny. Mrs Kinsale's place had its windows smashed in, just hours after you were sacked. So don't tell me you were half a mile away when you were seen with the brick in your hand. It won't wash.'

'It's still the truth,' said Daniel, whom anger and confusion had made stubborn. He made to get past Max, but his stepfather pulled him by the arm. 'I haven't finished with you!'

'Max!' cried Lisa, and there was a note in her voice that Max had never heard before; Daniel not for years. Lisa said steadily: 'Let him go. Whatever's happened, the morning is time enough.'

'Time enough to come up with a pack of fresh lies,' said Max. 'I want the truth now, while Gabriel Spicer's blood's fresh on his collar.'

'Sorry Max – nobody's blood there but my own,' said Daniel, with a curious smile. 'Group A, rhesus positive – check it out.' And he stood there smiling, and swaying, and smiling still: until at last Lisa saw that he was about to collapse, and rushing forward caught him as he fell.

The hospital was not high-rise, as Ruby had imagined, but a sprawling plantation of rural huts on the fringe of the city. Between each hut was a covered walkway where she wandered for some time before discovering the row of curtained cubicles in which Daniel sat waiting. She found him reading a book from the trolley, a thumbed airport novel with a broken doll on the cover. When he saw her he put it down and waved. His face was swollen like a berry.

'Don't worry,' said Daniel, seeing her expression. 'It's not catching.'

'You look awful,' said Ruby.

'Thanks.' His voice had acquired a slight lisp. Ruby was aware of a sudden fragility in his movements.

'I came as soon as I got Dad's message. Where are he and Lisa?'

'Getting themselves some awful coffee from a machine. You can have some too, I should think.'

'It's you I came to see.'

'Thanks, but there's no need. I'll be out of here as soon as they've done the paperwork. There's nothing much the matter with me.'

'That's not what I heard,' Ruby blurted. The question would not stay in any longer. 'What's this about you getting into a fight with Gabriel Spicer last night?'

'That wasn't me. Ask Gabriel yourself – he's in the next ward.'

'But Dad said—'

'I told you, it wasn't me!' snapped Daniel. 'All right?'

'No need to leap down my throat! If you say it wasn't you I believe you,' declared Ruby. 'You're not a liar,' she added, with a conviction that seemed to surprise him.

'Try telling Mum and Max. They're probably interviewing Gabriel right now, trying to get him to finger me.'

'You said they'd gone for coffee.'

'Whatever,' said Daniel, looking bored. He was gazing at the doll on the cover of his book. 'I wasn't there,' he added, more to himself than to Ruby.

A figure passed the open door at the end of the room. Through the frosted windows Ruby saw it hesitate, then retrace its steps. She vaguely recognised the girl, and could even make a stab at her name: June, Jane, or similar. The star of last year's school panto, where she'd made a winsome Cinderella. Now she wore black jeans and a bomber jacket, her long hair tucked inside the collar. Daniel still had not seen her, so engrossed had he become in his book's cover.

'Hello, Daniel,' said the girl. 'I've talked to Gabriel.'

Daniel stared. 'Jane? What are you doing here?'

'I told you. I was seeing Gabriel.'

The interest faded from Daniel's face. 'How is he?' he asked absently.

'He'll live. Do you care?'

Daniel paused to consider. 'Should I? He's not my favourite person, you understand?'

Jane shrugged. Her face was white. 'I don't like hospitals,' she said, slumping into the nearest chair.

— 144 —

'What does your friend have to say about last night?' Ruby asked Jane.

Jane looked questioningly at Daniel. 'It's all right,' he explained. 'Ruby's my sister. You could say we're related,' he added with a laugh. 'So tell us – what did Gabriel say?'

'I don't know how to begin,' said Jane. 'He wouldn't talk for a long time – not to his parents, nor the nurses. But Tom Lacey had been telling everyone how you'd clocked him with a brick, so they just thought – you know – he was ashamed to admit it, being twice your size and all.'

'But that wasn't it?' prompted Ruby.

'No, it wasn't. I know when Gabriel's lying, and he wasn't lying about this. When everyone else had left the room, he told me.' Jane lowered her voice: 'Whatever he saw out there, it terrified him.'

'*Whatever*?' repeated Ruby. 'What are you trying to say?'

'I'm not sure. Look, he wasn't making much sense. The concussion left him confused, the nurse told me.'

'And if it wasn't concussion? What does he *think* he saw?'

'Something muffled. From a distance it looked like you, Daniel. He called out – they all did, when they saw you (I mean *it*) about to smash that window. Then it started to run. The rest hung back, but Gabriel chased after and grabbed hold of it. They fell together, and rolled over and over on the ground, and – it's weird, but Gabriel says this thing had *ropes* hanging from its arms, long ropes of dripping weed, and as they rolled they began to wind themselves around him, till he could hardly breathe. It was like wrestling with a scarecrow. He thought he was drowning.'

'This creature,' said Daniel, who was listening gravely. 'Did he describe its face?'

'Its face?' Jane looked nervously to the door. 'Where the face should have been … It was *raw*. Red raw, and white with the bone underneath. And its breath stunk, a hiss with a jet of bubbles. And in the eye sockets—' She stopped short, and peered up at them. Ruby looked back, incredulous and pitying. Whatever terror had reduced Gabriel Spicer to silence, this girl had caught it like an infection. The truth must be several removes distant, at the far end of a chain of Chinese whispers. She observed Daniel's battered face, now nodding impassively as if nothing Jane had said was surprising. A nasty suspicion crossed her mind. Could it be that Daniel's face, twisted with anger and made unfamiliar by the street lights, might be taken for the nightmare of Jane's description? While she considered it, Daniel spoke.

'So Gabriel's put me in the clear?'

'Yes, he has,' said Jane. Then she added: 'Is that really the most important thing to you?'

'You're not the one about to be arrested for assault,' Daniel pointed out. 'I'm sure Gabriel will recover. Especially with you to mop his brow,' he added pointedly.

'What do you mean?'

'Now you're back together, I mean. No, it's all right, there's no need to get offended. Meg told me.'

'We're not together anymore,' said Jane, recovering quickly. 'As of tonight, we're finished.'

Daniel smiled a little, despite his lip. 'You're hard to keep up with. What brought this on?'

'He told me about what happened in the underpass,'

—— 146 ——

said Jane. 'I don't like bullies. I thought he'd grown out of that.'

'Perhaps he has, now.'

'Jane!' a voice called sharply. Jane twisted, and the others looked to see Mr Garfield standing in the doorway, with his raincoat draped over his arm like a bull-fighter's cape. His hair was carefully parted, with a neat tie knotted high above his collar, but anger shone from him. 'Jane,' he commanded again. 'Come here right now.'

Without a word Jane rose, and made her way to her father. An apologetic smile touched the brink of her lip, not quite spilling into words. As she left the ward they saw Mr Garfield catch her by the elbow. An '*I thought I told you*' reached them from the corridor before the rattle of drugs from a passing trolley drowned the pair.

'Well, what did you make of that?' asked Ruby, turning to her stepbrother. Daniel had been staring at the door dazedly, but at her question stirred himself, and even reached in a haphazard way for his neglected book.

'Either Gabriel's developed an imagination after all these years,' he said, 'or that knock on the head has made him see things.' He spoke in a cynical voice Ruby knew too well to trust.

'Maybe,' she said, then hesitated. 'Unless Jane was telling us the truth.'

Daniel turned on her, suddenly furious. 'You don't believe that! Why do you say that? Are you trying to give me the creeps?'

'No, I didn't mean to,' Ruby stumbled.

'Because I've already *got* the creeps, all right? So take your mind games and play them on someone else.'

Then Ruby saw – and cursed herself for blindness –

that Daniel too was terrified. She went to his side and took his bruised face tenderly in her hands. 'It's all right,' she said. 'Everything's going to be fine.'

'I can't help it,' croaked Daniel, not hiding any longer. 'He is my brother after all. Part of my brother is in him. In *it*.'

'Daniel, you don't have to talk about this.'

'I've spent too long not talking! We all have. But this isn't something you can bottle up, is it? He's out there! It's happening, and now not just to me. Timon—'

'Shh!' She cradled his head, his cheeks in her cupped hands. 'You're in shock, you know.'

'Timon is desperate. The way he is now, he's a fish out of water, a freak. He can't last. There's no point to him, he knows it. Soon they'll come for him. The Lockermen—'

'Hush, hush.'

'I think he'll panic. He'll do something, something vicious. This thing last night, you can see how it turned out. He was trying to prove something to me, with Gabriel and old Mrs Kinsale. As if that could make things better! What will he do now?'

Lisa and Max had been in the room for some seconds, unnoticed.

'Shh,' said Ruby.

'I'll tell you. He'll go further next time. Next time it won't be casualty, it'll be the morgue. He's going to make someone pay. That's the way he's always been.'

'That's enough.'

'Watch your back, Ruby.'

'That's enough. Look, Mum and Dad are here.'

And with a small, throat-clearing cough Max came forward, a plastic cup of awful coffee steaming in each hand.

Thirteen

*I*T WAS FIVE DAYS LATER. RUBY WAS ALONE AT
HOME, unless one counted Aunt Jenkins slumbering
near the fire – and Ruby didn't. To her, Aunt Jenkins
was an object, one requiring more care than most, like
an awkward-to-dust piece of china. To *be* Aunt Jenkins
– it did not bear thinking about. Besides, Ruby had her
own problems. The study door was ajar, and through it
she could see her revision schedule. Each day was
assigned a line of pencilled tasks, and against the first
few days a gratifying tick had been added in red marker
pen. But the last three weeks were bare. Tomorrow she
had to return north, get the coach to her hilltop city.
Tomorrow – and two weeks later there would be end-
of-year exams, which she now knew she would fail. All
work had ceased.

Vacations ought not to be like this. Ruby felt vacated
herself: hollow, and apt to be blown by the first breeze.
It was a strange sensation. She would have liked a cup
of tea, but could not bring herself to make it, or even to
shoo the fly from her arm. With the habit of mind she
had been trained in she observed herself. Her ambi-
tions were still there, hung up like corks from a bush
hat. To leave Morton's Holt with a first-class degree.
To impress Dad. To make money, yet not become its
slave. But the words no longer drove her: they were just

quotations. Valentine would not stick by her, anyway. And on her own, how would she cope?

'Look at him! Bold as brass!' announced Aunt Jenkins abruptly. Ruby stared at the old woman, who was suddenly sitting bolt upright in her chair. She was gazing straight ahead, eyes wide with excitement. The potted fern on the table by her side smashed onto the tiles, and sent soil spilling across Ruby's feet.

'Go back to sleep, you've been dreaming again,' said Ruby, rousing herself to the thought of clearing up the mess.

But Aunt Jenkins was rigid, and would not sit back. 'Tell him to go away! He's got no business here!'

Ruby looked around helplessly, but she was alone. Her father and Lisa had gone for Lisa's eighteen-week scan. Daniel, who had been inseparable from Lisa for the last few days, had gone with them. Hospital was becoming a habit.

'Don't do this now!' cried Ruby in panic, for Aunt Jenkins had begun to tremble uncontrollably. Was she having some sort of fit? Ruby wouldn't know what to do. She snatched at the half-remembered advice she had picked up from public information films at school. The airway! Got to keep the airway clear, remove dentures, make sure she doesn't swallow her own tongue!

But Aunt Jenkins was not having a fit. After a few moments her back relaxed, and eased into the curve of her chair, and her breathing became steady. Her gaze did not leave the window overlooking the garden, however. Ruby followed it to the shade at the far end of the lawn, where the laurel hedge met the first cluster of small trees – the magnolia, and a group of cherries that had lost their blossom to the storms. Underneath one of them, casually dressed in a green woollen jersey, stood a young man. He was waving at her.

'It isn't right,' said Aunt Jenkins tetchily. 'He always did want to break the rules. Can't you make him go away?'

'Who?' said Ruby, forcing herself to look from the window. This was not happening: there was nothing to see.

'Timon, of course! Can't you see him? He's been pestering us for weeks, now. He needs sending about his business.'

'You're imagining things, Aunt Jenkins. Let me turn the radiator down – you're getting very hot.'

'Stop fussing over me! It's him you should be dealing with!' Aunt Jenkins was getting agitated again. 'He'll bring us all trouble, especially now the hunger's on him. Can't you feel it? The tide pulling?'

'You're feverish – there's nothing out there.' Ruby turned her back to the window, seeing to Aunt Jenkins. She was getting frightened despite herself. Blast these superstitions! 'Daniel has been putting these ideas in your head, hasn't he?'

'Daniel is as ignorant as you. He won't be told – no one will.'

The shaking was as bad as ever now. Ruby fumbled with the top button of Aunt Jenkins' blouse. Then there was a noise from behind them: fingers scratching, scraping at the window. Ruby span round, and saw with the corner of her eye something that was already only half-there: a leering face, with its nose flattened against the glass. Its mouth was a slobber of lips, a smile from which the top and bottom teeth were missing.

She sprang to the window. She heard feet running,

but there was nothing to see. The fresh soil on the ground below was undisturbed. She pulled up the sash, and felt the breeze come in cool and fresh. But a dripping strand of weed had wound itself across the latch.

'Stay there, Aunt Jenkins.'

'Where are you going?' Aunt Jenkins asked, with a quiver in her voice. 'You're not leaving me alone, are you?'

'Someone's having a joke with us. I'm going to sort this out, once and for all.' Ruby's face was white.

'Stay with me!' cried Aunt Jenkins in rising panic. 'You don't know what you're doing.'

'I'll be back in five minutes. Less. Just sit tight.'

And Ruby was already out of the conservatory door.

Lisa and Max held hands across the bench in the Sister's room. Max's nervousness showed in the jokes he felt obliged to make about the adverts in *Mother and Baby* magazine; Lisa's in the little, sneeze-like laughs with which she greeted them. Beneath, though, lay unshakable happiness. Watching from the door, Daniel envied them. Happiness – bright and hard as a billiard ball. Was this what it was, to love without condition?

'I'm glad you came, darling,' Lisa smiled, looking round at him. She held out her hand to Daniel. 'Come on, don't hover – sit with us.'

Daniel came and sat. To his surprise Max shuffled over to make room.

'So, have you been thinking?' Max asked him.

'Thinking what?'

'About a name, of course!'

'A name? No!'

'You should then. We've been working on our shortlist.'

'I'm not sure this is the time,' said Lisa, checking her watch nervously.

'Why not? Daniel has a right to his say, the same as anyone. What do you reckon, Daniel?'

'I don't mind, honestly. What's in a name?'

'Exactly, so long as it's healthy,' agreed Lisa.

'"So long as it's healthy." I think that's become your Mum's new catch phrase,' Max mocked. 'Aunt Jenkins' contribution, if you'll believe it, was Ichabod. Fancy expecting the child to carry that through life.'

The Sister returned, and asked Lisa to lie on a bed. Lisa pulled her shirt up, and the Sister smeared her abdomen with some kind of jelly, then moved a scanner across her skin, while on the monitor a blur of lights and shades resolved itself into a womb. Something was throbbing.

'I can't see,' Max complained. Lisa, watching the screen from her bed, said nothing, but a watery grin began to spread across her face.

'Let's see if it will change position,' said the Sister, and moved the scanner again. This time the picture on the screen made sense. Looking over Max's shoulder Daniel saw a bulbous head, and a body curled like an apostrophe.

'Oh, I can see its arm!' cried Lisa. 'Look, Max!'

'I see it,' breathed Max. He reached out and squeezed Lisa's hand. At once the foetus gave a start. The limbs clutched.

'It felt you! Did you see?' asked Lisa.

'It looked terrified, poor thing. What a world to come into!' said Max with sudden feeling.

'Oh, Max!'

'The ultrasound seems to stimulate them,' the Sister explained.

'They don't feel any distress, do they?'

'It's an automatic response,' said the Sister briskly. 'They're not aware of anything.'

'Daniel, can you see from where you're standing?'

'I can see fine,' said Daniel, not coming closer. The sight fascinated him, but was disconcerting. That little frog-like clutch of tubes and tissues was destined to be a person, like him. He too had once been just such a pulsating thing. It was easy to know this – but impossible to believe. And anyway, what did it mean?

It meant one thing, at least. This was the child he had set himself to protect from Timon. That was why he had become Lisa's unsuspected bodyguard. He feared what his brother might do against a life so vulnerable, so *succulent* – how he might try to leave his mark. Timon had known about his little sister, had cradled her in a sneer that was more than half a threat. He must be ready. Watch – that was the task. Watch and wait.

'It seems as though you're going to have a little boy, Mr and Mrs Hilliard,' the Sister said.

'What?' exclaimed Daniel. 'A boy? Are you sure?'

'Daniel!' Lisa laughed.

'You can see for yourself,' said the Sister, indicating the screen. 'We can't be one hundred per cent certain till we get the results of the amniocentesis, but in this case …'

Daniel stared. The child on the screen, with stubby arms and outsize head, was at home in its own small universe. *I've got my place*, it seemed to say. Though helpless, it did not need him. 'A boy?' Daniel repeated stupidly. Standing there in the hospital, he was filled with misgiving, a bitter feeling seeping up from his stomach. Not that there had been no danger, but that it was elsewhere, and beyond him. Where was his sister? It never occurred to him that Timon might be lying, or mistaken. Only that he had been tricked, and for the last time, and in a way he did not even now understand.

From somewhere down the corridor, somewhere very far away, he thought he heard a woman scream.

The magnolia tree had become a candelabra. Waxy, skyward-pointing buds thronged it, each white and strung with threads of pink. Here, she thought, he must have stood. Or near here – perhaps a pace or two further on to the lawn. Ruby went to the spot, and looked from it to the window of the living-room. It was dark: Aunt Jenkins was invisible. She glanced up to her own bedroom. The corner of her wardrobe could just be made out, and the draped sheen of her yellow silk dress over the wooden chair back. From here he could have seen little, even by day; nothing by moonlight. Yet his gaze, the sense that she had been *recognised*, yes and mocked too, by a stranger who saw into her and through her, still burned her cheek. Terror she had felt at first, and anger; and now a kind of bewilderment. Ten minutes' search of the garden had given her no kind of clue. She wondered at herself, and at the wish she had to see him again. To tell him what she thought of him, of course – and to sort out in her mind whose face his face recalled for her. Was it Timon's after all?

Once, Ruby had formed a theory about this man. He was some chancer, most likely an acquaintance of Timon's. He had heard about Lisa's remarriage, and Max's money, and seized on a likeness to try and pose as Timon, to insinuate himself into the family. It would not be hard to concoct a story, and pick up a few plausible details. No doubt that was why he had been hanging round the house – spying. And if he could not approach Lisa directly (what mother would not know her own son?) he could at least work on Daniel, who had been a child when Timon died. If played on cleverly Daniel might be brought to believe. Get Daniel on his side, and then …

But it would not do. Daniel had no power over Max: what would be the use of befriending *him*? She sighed, dismissed the whole convoluted scheme, and stamped impatiently towards the wood.

A voice said: 'Did someone sigh for love?'

There was a tinkling of laughter which ran the length of the laurel with the wind, and set the bright leaf-scales like glass cymbals beating. The hedge-snake curled slightly. Ruby froze. It was not a voice she knew, though something in it stirred her.

'Who's there?' she called.

Again there was the scuffling of feet, and this time Ruby thought she had narrowed down its source – to the thinnest part of the hedge, where a rogue bush had pushed aside the laurel, then shrivelled into barren ground. As she peered through, she was aware of movement beyond the hedge. A gloved hand? A patch of jumper? Someone moving, fast.

'Who's there?' she called again.

'Your well-wisher,' said the voice, with a grin in it. 'Shall we touch fingers through the hedge? Don't back away – our eyes at least should meet.'

Then with a yelp of fright Ruby saw him, though she did not think he had moved. But the hedge shifted itself slightly, and in amongst its branches she found herself staring into a face which was all leaf-mould and owl-shadow. It was the green man of Daniel's drawing, to the life. The forehead was lightly veined, above yellow eyes that did not pierce but enveloped her like slow honey.

She felt herself wanting to whimper in terror, but managed some bravado: 'I know who you are – you're the creep who's been hanging round the house.'

The round, owl eyes blinked. The lids were feathered with lashes, the skin above discoloured as if bruised. Ruby felt the confidence drain from her. They were not human eyes, for all their cunning. Her theory about a gold-digger melted in the crucible of their gentle heat. Something trembled within her, and in the air above.

'You know better than that,' said the voice, not unkindly. 'We're almost related. You could be my sister. My stepmother too, perhaps. Watch closely – I'll show you a trick.'

Again the owl eyes blinked. But now their lids were yellow, not blue; the yellow of autumn leaves. And leaves were what those eyes had become: two dry discs, hanging from the dead bush in the hedge. The face which had been holding her gaze was gone.

Ruby stepped backwards, almost stumbling in her haste. She was shocked, frightened, but also sharply aware how ridiculous she looked, crouching in conversation with a laurel. She glanced round to see if there was a watcher in the garden behind. No – but someone out of sight was running lightly back into the wood. She could hear the footfalls on the leafy ground, and a fresh peal of laughter receding. And after all it was Daniel's laugh. A trick! A stupid prank, and she had fallen for it! Anger drove out her fear. Daniel was to blame for this. He was just as crazy as they said, and malicious with it. He had crept behind the hedge to frighten her. He could have given her a heart attack!

'Daniel! I'll make you pay for that!'

Ruby ran after.

She did not pause to consider those owl eyes, or how hard it would be for Daniel to play that kind of trick in daylight. Had she stopped for a moment, she might have thought how subtly different was Daniel's voice from the one that had just spoken to her. She might have wondered how the laurel hedge had moved, or what seeds those gold-flecked eyes had planted in her mind, and how quickly they grew. She might have feared whatever waited for her in the shade of Morton's Wood – a thing that could seem like a tree, or a man, with spiny fingers and a light footfall.

Instead she walked, then ran after, and found her steps growing softer with each pace, until she seemed to be floating into the wood on a current. At last – too late – she realised that she could not stop. She tried, but her legs would not obey. She was still hurtling forward. She felt herself pulled on by the undertow, forward through the trees and down out of sunlight.

She screamed.

And the sound snagged itself in the leafless canopy, and hung there.

They returned from the hospital. Max amused himself by treating Lisa like porcelain, stepping smartly to open her passenger door while she was still fumbling with her purse.

'Daniel, can you bring the bag in?' asked Lisa.

'Sure.'

They crunched over the gravel, Max pacing ahead

with the front door keys. But Daniel was first into the house.

'Hello?' called Daniel from the hall, to the house in general. He had been hoping to sound natural, but couldn't rein in his anxiety. Even Max noticed.

'Steady on, Daniel. We've only been away a couple of hours.'

There was a low moan from the living-room, which Daniel for a moment thought must have come from the throat of an animal. But it ended with Lisa's name.

Lisa pushed past him. Entering the living-room they saw Aunt Jenkins sprawled on her chair. She was sleeping, but no ordinary sleep. Some violent apprehension made her limbs tremble, and that first long moan of fear was followed by others, in which Lisa's name sometimes broke surface, sometimes Ruby's. Lisa knelt beside her, chafing her hand.

'Aunt Jenkins! Wake up!'

'Should I get the doctor?' asked Max.

'Yes, yes!' cried Lisa. 'Aunt Jenkins?'

Aunt Jenkins opened her eyes. 'Tolly, Timon, and now this … It's too awful.'

'What's too awful? Answer me, will you?' cried Lisa.

'Ruby. She's gone.'

'Gone? Where? Did she say?'

'She's *gone*,' repeated Aunt Jenkins, with emphasis.

Daniel was already on the upstairs landing, making for Ruby's room. The door knob cracked against the wall as he slammed it open. Ruby's duvet was folded neatly on the bed. Her drawers and cupboard doors were open.

'Ruby?' Daniel asked, in a quiet voice.

No one answered. The clock by her bed moved imperturbably on. 'Oh no,' he said. 'Not Ruby.'

He felt her pillow. It was damp. Damp footsteps trailed across the carpet, to and from the window and the door. Droplets had formed on the plastic CD holder screwed into the wall.

'Mum! Max!'

Max came up. 'Where's Ruby?' he demanded.

Daniel's face met him, blank and scared. Just then the red digits on Ruby's clock-radio flipped to five-thirty. There was a click, and almost immediately an acoustic guitar strummed, with folk accompaniment. Daniel immediately recognized Lisa's farewell album, *Shallow Breath*. His mother's voice flooded the room.

Don't come looking. I'm where you'll never find me.
Don't try understanding – if you could I'd still be here.
I walked out of your life, so bolt the door behind me.
Pretend you never cried a single tear.

'What's going on?' Max asked, of the song as much as of Daniel.

'She must have hooked the alarm to her CD player,' said Daniel, dazed.

'I don't mean that! Where's Ruby? Do you know anything about this?'

'No, nothing,' Daniel said, which was almost true. But he was beginning to think that he should have known, and much sooner.

'Where's all her stuff? She couldn't carry it by herself. She must have got someone to help her. Unless ...' Max spotted the portable phone in the corner. He switched it on and pressed Redial.

'Hello? Who am I speaking to, please? ... Redfern cabs?' A minute later he slammed the phone down. 'She took a taxi to the bus station, half an hour ago.'

'The bus station?' echoed Daniel. It sounded so ordinary that his anxiety of a few moments before suddenly seemed overblown. 'Do you think she's going back to college a day early?'

'She's not going alone, wherever it is. There was a man with her. It was him who made the call.'

Daniel tensed. 'What sort of man? Was he young?'

'I don't know! But I'm going to find out. They may still be there. You stay and help your mum with Aunt Jenkins. I'll take the car.'

'I'm coming with you,' declared Daniel. Max opened his mouth to protest, then conceded: 'It may take two.'

The doctor's car was already drawing into the drive just as they came downstairs. Lisa, standing in the doorway, kept casting backward glances to where Aunt Jenkins sat white-faced, but sipping now at some sugary tea.

'I heard the music. Why is she playing that song?' she asked.

Max told her what they'd found, but Lisa seemed not to take it in: 'Valentine wrote it for me, did you know? His way of dropping a hint ... Oh Max! You don't think Val ... Oh, what are we going to do?'

Max took her hand. 'We're going to find Ruby and bring her back, that's what. Look, here's Dr Dukakis. Hello, doctor, the patient's just through here.' He kissed Lisa. 'It'll be all right, you'll see. We'll find her.'

Dr Dukakis exuded unflustered authority. Within seconds she had taken Lisa back to the living room, and engaged her in a series of quiet questions concerning Aunt Jenkins, who by this time had begun to deplore the fuss being made of her.

Released, Max put his Rover into gear. The five

miles to the city centre were a gradual accumulation of concrete, from the fragile countryside of Morton's Holt, through a complex maze of rat-runs, then onto the ring road. Max swore at the traffic lights and jumped a pelican crossing, before swerving dramatically into the bus station.

'What if we've missed her?' Daniel asked. 'What if she won't come?'

'She'll come. I'm not having her go off like this, without a word. Look at the state she left Aunt Jenkins in.'

Daniel did not reply. There was more to this, he knew, than Max could guess at. More than he could tell now and be believed. Timon had been clever, as always. Ruby might be the perfect victim, with her stock of unknown and untraceable friends from college, her unpredictable resolves, her various forms of pride. She could, if she chose, quite easily make herself disappear. No one would understand it: but then no one expected to understand Ruby.

Max parked in the disabled bay at the front of the station. A coach to London was reversing to leave. Daniel leapt out of the car and searched its windows, but Ruby was not there.

Max strode to the ticket office. 'When does the Durham coach leave?'

'There's no Durham coach today,' the assistant informed him. 'It runs twice a week: Mondays and Thursdays.'

'Are you sure?' rapped out Max.

The assistant allowed himself a small smile. 'I should think I am, sir. Are you interested in buying a ticket?'

Max stormed back, and began to search the

queues that had formed at each of the coach bays. He looked into the bookshop. He asked the women coming out of the ladies' toilet if they had seen a girl matching Ruby's description.

At last he came back to Daniel.

'No sign of her. Listen, and think carefully. Has Ruby mentioned any friends from university? Special friends – people she might go and stay with?'

'No. No, there's been no one.'

Max left him again, and Daniel wandered through the back entrance where the luggage trolleys were lined against the wall. Here was a steep side street, and a taxi rank. A Redfern cab was parked just in front of him, waiting for a fare. Had Ruby been inside just half an hour ago? Had Timon? He hesitated, wondering whether to speak to the driver, who was reading a newspaper and flicking ash from his window. How could Timon have persuaded her to leave the house so suddenly?

He knocked on the cab window. The driver looked up, and threw his cigarette into the gutter. 'Where to, son?'

Daniel explained about the fare from Morton's Holt. He was looking for a brother and a sister.

'Brother and sister?' laughed the cabbie. 'I'm losing my touch. I had them down for lovers.'

'Then you have seen them? Did she say where she was going?'

'Are you joking? I couldn't get a word out of her the whole journey. He was the gabby one … But no – he just told me to go to the bus station. Hang on – isn't that her now?'

Daniel looked where the man was pointing, up the hill to a sharp corner in the road, where a streetlight illuminated the retreating backs of three people, two men and a woman. The clothes they wore, and the short-haired lurcher at their heels, made him think of the shopping arcade – of the sleeping bags and cardboard petitions, where he had once dropped a pound coin into a dead boy's palm. One of them was wearing Ruby's coat.

'Thanks,' he said to the cabbie, as he began to climb the steep street, catapulting himself around the corner with the aid of the lamp-post. Almost at once he was in the midst of the group. They had stopped while one of the men knelt to give the dog a piece of liquorice. The woman looking on was lean, with a face pinched and colourless. She was not Ruby. But from the back she might have been mistaken for Ruby: a Ruby whose life had been blighted. Over her patched jeans she wore a coat that looked incongruously new, and thick for the winter. Daniel recognised it, and remembered how Ruby had mocked Max's safe choice: it had been her father's Christmas present.

'Where did you get that coat?' Daniel blurted breathlessly, stumbling to a halt beside her.

The woman looked at him with a frown, and drew the coat closer. 'Who wants to know?'

'It's my sister's. Where did you get it?'

'What are you accusing her of?' asked the second man, moving to stand protectively beside her. 'It's not stolen.'

'That's right – it had already been dumped.'

'Dumped?'

'You heard – we found it in a skip. What do you care anyway?'

'I'm not interested in the coat! I just want to find the girl who owns it.'

There was silence. 'Why do you want to find her?' asked the man with the dog at last. He stood up, and the dog climbed up to beat its forelegs on his thighs. The man's eyes were quick and suspicious.

'I think she's in danger,' said Daniel.

'There's too many people interfering in other people's lives.'

'Drop it, Mike,' said the woman. 'You can see he's not faking it.' She shook herself free of the other man, and said to Daniel: 'In a skip down by the sandbanks, near the Exhibition Centre. We saw her throw the coat in, maybe fifteen minutes ago.'

Daniel stared at her. 'Did you say the sandbanks?'

'You know it?'

A choking feeling was rising in Daniel's throat. He nodded.

'You OK?' asked the woman.

Daniel was backing away, down the hill. He could no longer speak. His half-guesses had been right after all – yet he had still done nothing that might have saved Ruby. He had been worse than stupid.

As he turned, he was dimly aware of Max standing on the street below him, looking up at the woman with the dog. But Daniel was already running back past the cab and the bus station towards the harbour. Quarter of an hour had passed since Ruby was seen there, time enough to walk a mile in any direction. It was a slim, hopeless lead. Had she been alone then, or still with Timon? He had been too slow-witted to ask.

Emerging from the old streets he hit a wall of silence and open sky, where the paving stones turned to cobble and the air to salt. A small, distant breathing was the sound of the infant sea. He had come to the sandbanks, a place where the ocean stretched one claw to scratch at the land's loose skin. A silted dead-end, useless for larger boats, except where the river scored a black channel through its centre. The wharfs were silent, under warehouses that rose in a sheer cliff of brick to shade them from the city's orange sky-glow. A few small craft still moored there, and there were iron ladders leading down from the wharf to reach them; but half their existence was spent on land, lopsided on the tidal sands. When the tide came it was with currents of savage strength.

Ruby was beneath one of the ladders. Her knees were tucked up under her chin. Daniel climbed down beside her. She was alone. Her skin, under the hand he reached out to her, was cold as glass.

'I'm cold, Daniel. So cold.'

'Ruby, come away from here – it's dangerous.' The tide had already begun to creep in amongst the sand pools.

'Everywhere's dangerous. Don't you know that?'

A gust pushed the water up to breach the nearest spar of sand. A quicksilver trickle flooded the shallow gulley near to Ruby's feet.

'Come back now, with me. It's not too late.'

'It was always too late. I know that now. When you've seen what *he* made me see.'

'And what was that? What did my waste of a brother show you?'

For the first time Ruby looked up at him. Her eyes, under the warehouse floodlight, were flat and glazed. She mouthed an answer, but Daniel heard no sound. A strange inversion had taken place. He seemed to be seeing Ruby's face in reflection, or behind the surface of a clear pane of water, which no words could penetrate. His skin prickled, but not with cold, and he found himself backing from her. Then she lifted her arms, till now clasped to her side. He saw the long ropes of weed that hung dripping from her wrists, ropes which extended down into the sand. Her hands were white and skeletal. At last a sound came: a guttural, bleeding hiss, squeezed from ruined lungs.

'He showed me this!'

At that Ruby collapsed into herself, chin hitting her chest and her arms rag-limp. The ropes of weed were gone. The horror of the moment dissipated, like the sickly smell that seemed suddenly to have surrounded them. Daniel recognised it, from the poisoned water of Morton's Pond. He began to understand a little. Was that what *he* had been meant to see, when Timon showed him his reflection? A vision of his own death? Of Death with a capital D?

Ruby was motionless on the sand. If he left her now, the sea would come, and in half an hour or less she would be submerged to her waist. An hour, and the frozen currents would ease her gently from the sand-bed where she sat half-sleeping. Her mouth would begin to bubble out sea water. Her clothes would drag her down.

He lifted her under the arms, and heaved her back up the sand to the bottom of the iron ladder. She was heavy. He had not realised how great the dead weight of a human being could be. Though she was too far gone now to struggle, it would be impossible to carry her to safety. He had achieved only a few minutes respite, before the water lapped against the stones of the quay.

He shouted: 'Help us! Help us, please!'

But the music from a pub at the front of the warehouse tore his voice to shreds.

There was nothing else to do. Cumbrously he knelt, lifted Ruby's body onto his own, and staggered to his feet. Immediately she began to slither down his back.

'Ruby! You've got to hang on!'

'Mmm?'

She was dreaming. 'Daniel! Do you have to?' she chided him sleepily.

'Just wake up,' he said, and again threaded his arms under hers. He began the painful climb up the ladder, holding her between him and it. She was trying to help, lifting one leg on to the bottom rung and straightening her body. But her fingers would not grip the rail, and once more she tipped back and sideways. This time she fell badly. One arm was trapped beneath her stomach and she moaned a little as the breath was knocked from her. Then she lay still.

'Ruby?' Daniel knelt on the sand beside her. Ruby's face was turned towards the water. Her eyes were open slightly. In the light of them he saw the tide foaming.

He looked behind him, to find the harbour alive with lights. A thousand lanterns were bobbing, just beneath the surface of the swirling water. By them a thousand heads were waiting: balloon-shaped heads, with nostrils flaring, bodies thin as famine. At that moment he felt the sea stream in over his foot. He shook it off as though it had bitten him, and, looking back, found that the lanterns were reflections from the floodlit far harbour. Ruby had taken hold of his ankle.

'I think I've lost it, Daniel,' she said flatly.

'Can you walk?' he asked. At once he was on his feet, and taking her by the arm. 'Just a few steps, and we'll be safe.'

Someone had appeared at the top of the ladder. Daniel saw with surprise that it was Max. He was shouting down, asking if Ruby were injured.

'She's not good,' he called back, then turned again to Ruby. 'Can you make it, Ruby?'

Her head moved, what might have been a nod. A few seconds later Max was on the sand too. He rubbed at Ruby's frozen hand.

'She's freezing. What's she doing down here?'

'I think – I don't know,' Daniel said, and shook his head.

'Well thank God you found her. Those people by the bus station said you'd come this way. Ruby love, can you talk?'

Between them he and Daniel helped Ruby to the ladder. It was a slow climb, with a wait on each rung for Ruby to get her breath back. Max held one hand from above; Daniel followed, ready to steady her should she fall. Swathes of black seaweed hung from the stones beside them. Below, the sea had reached the harbour wall.

Max made the quay, then reached down and pulled Ruby clear of the ladder. By the time Daniel joined him, Max had taken off his coat and laid it across her. He looked up, his face stricken.

'She's barely conscious. You'd better get help.'

Daniel stared down at Ruby's dark lips and felt

her rib-cage tremble under the coat. She was saying something repeatedly, mumbling.

'I think I've lost the baby. You don't understand. I think it's gone.'

'Shh, you're safe now.' Daniel held her, as she had held him once, cupping her wet cheeks. 'Ruby, Ruby. You know I love you, don't you?'

'Daniel, go for help!' instructed Max.

Her face was cold. There was a brittle smile on it. She took his hand.

'Brother, I know it,' she said, and closed her eyes.

Fourteen

*I*T WAS EARLY MAY, AND LISA WAS GLANCING regretfully at her summer wardrobe. Very little of it would do: by the time the hot weather came she'd have outgrown it. The summer was a time of dim dread: the largeness, the heat, the discomfort of a baby weighing her down through August. There was so much she had forgotten since she had carried Daniel. Meanwhile, garden duties demanded her attention, duties for which she already felt unfit. She could no longer face turning the soil, was barely up to weeding borders. Yet the garden plan that had formed in her mind over the last month seemed ever more urgent. And so, as they were dressing, she announced to Max her new resolve.

'That laurel hedge,' she began. 'I don't think it belongs here.'

'Mmm?' Max responded. A silk tie hung from his neck, with a pattern of mermaids and winkles.

'It was Val's idea – I never liked it. It makes the garden look so much smaller, don't you think? I'd rather have a rose-bed. Max, are you listening?'

'Whatever you think's best,' replied Max, who wasn't. For the third time he attempted to get the ends of his tie to hang at more appropriate lengths. A handsome silver clip waited on the side table, ready to grip the plush silk. 'Do you suppose they'll send the TV people this afternoon?'

'I really don't know, Max.'

'After all, the Exhibition Centre is quite a big deal. All that Lottery money ...'

'Then I'm sure they will.' Lisa had not chosen the best time to interest Max in horticulture. But there was something else she knew she had to say.

'That pond in the woods, too – I really think we should fill it in. It's hardly more than a puddle in summer, and the mud's putrid. Especially if there are to be young children running about, the place just isn't safe.'

At that Max grunted. '*Children*? Children plural? Does that mean you've come round to the idea—'

'Of Val's child living here?' said Lisa. She sighed, and put her arms out to him. 'If Ruby really wants to keep it, I'm hardly going to throw her out of the house, now am I?'

Max came over and embraced her. He was truly grateful for this oblique permission. 'Ruby needs all our help now.'

'I know that. And I'm not out to take revenge on the unborn, whatever she may think. But she has no idea what it's going to be like – the responsibility of a baby, at her age.'

'She's very young,' nodded Max. 'And she's been through a lot. It's a miracle the baby survived at all. I think in some way she took that as a kind of sign.'

'Perhaps,' said Lisa. 'Perhaps it is one.' She wandered to the window, absent-mindedly straightening the sleeve of her jersey.

A thought occurred to Max. 'You know, I wonder if we should move altogether? This house is full of memories for you – and how many of them good ones?'

'No, no,' she said vaguely. 'That's not it.' She looked down at the lawn, and the wood beyond it, now just pricking into leaf. Morton's Holt. This was her home, her centre. 'It's our place, Max. A place for all of us. We have to make it right, now.'

A premonition fluttered through her mind.

'We're going to be so happy here.'

Daniel and Ruby were sitting in the conservatory, at either end of a hammock-like sofa heavy with cushions.

'What did you see? Tell me. Did you see Timon?'

Ruby said nothing, but took hold of one of the ropes and tilted back dangerously.

'Careful!' cried Daniel. 'Those tiles are hard!'

'You worry too much,' said Ruby. 'My head is harder – I've proved that much if I've proved anything.'

'But Ruby!'

'Don't worry, little brother. You asked a question. Did I see Timon? Well, what do you think?'

'I think you've been avoiding the subject for weeks now.'

'Timon's not the only subject worth talking about,' said Ruby crisply.

'I know, I know.'

'I thought I'd had a miscarriage, remember?'

'Yes, I was there. But look, Aunt Jenkins says he's gone. And since then I've not – well, I've not *sensed* him round every corner. I think he's disappeared. But you know for sure, don't you?'

Ruby stood up from the sofa, and went to look at the

garden, where a light drizzle had just begun. The pit-pat rain stroked the glass in the conservatory roof.

'He knew they were going to find him. He never had any hope for himself – he just wanted to scratch his name onto the world. That's what I was meant to be, an epitaph. A way of writing TIMON WAS HERE.'

'He chose a funny way to do it.'

'I've hardly stopped laughing since. Oh, never mind. To take a life, or make it – what's the difference? Val's way or his?'

'A big difference, I should say,' replied Daniel with conviction.

'Well, perhaps you're right.'

He smiled ruefully. 'Did I tell you? When we found you were gone, Mum thought Val had come to whisk you back to Durham.'

'Really?' said Ruby. 'Perhaps I'd have let him, if he had.'

'You'd have had more sense.'

'You're much too kind,' said Ruby.

Daniel still had not got a straight answer. 'But it *was* Timon in the taxi with you, wasn't it?'

'Yes, yes. Oh, I knew he was a ghost, of course. I was more than half a ghost myself. All the way from Morton's Holt, I saw it with his eyes. The spring leaves already yellow, all those bustling people hooped and pale. Death in everything. One woman, I remember – she was so immaculate, dressed in pure Armani! But just a pace behind her walked a shadow, with a tumour on her neck, and a face half eaten …'

Ruby stopped, and looked at her own hands, red from the rope's friction. Automatically she began to wind the chain from her neck about her finger. Never, since Daniel had known her, had she mentioned her mother's illness.

'When we got out of the car, my eyes were bad. I could hardly see where I was going, and I had to lean on him. He brought me down to the docks. All the time he was saying terrible things about Valentine. "My Darling Valentine," he would sing, and laugh. You know the kind of laugh I mean. He said, what did I need a brand new coat for, throw it in the skip, so I did. And he said, kick off your shoes, so I kicked them off into the harbour. And then, sit yourself on the sand and let the sea take you. So I sat down on the wet sand and he walked on towards the water.' She shrugged.

'You never saw him after that?'

'No. But he wasn't alone.' Ruby came back from the window and took her place with Daniel again. Her locket chain was a helix of twisted gold. 'There was … *something* following him. A man, I suppose – but at first I thought it belonged on four legs. I thought it had just raised itself to sniff the air. My eyesight was blurred, I told you. But I remember a white head, and a flat face, and the rest was wrapped in strips of cloth which dragged after it. I saw it gleam in the moonlight. A long, white slug.'

Daniel remembered his own sight of the Lockermen, and Timon's terror of them.

'Timon knew it was there?'

'He wasn't running away. But yes, I think he knew. There were others waiting for him, up ahead. There was nowhere for him to go.'

All this time Aunt Jenkins had been sitting in the conservatory, shielded by ferns from Daniel and Ruby. She was only lightly asleep, and their conversation fed her dreams. Young Daniel, how his voice resembled

Tolly's! And Valentine's fingers, how clever they were! But how hard his fist. A frown crossed Aunt Jenkins' sleeping face. Timon had entered her dream, uninvited. He was slinking across the lawn in a long, mud-trailing coat, and didn't look himself at all. There's one in every family, Aunt Jenkins thought sagely. She opened her eyes for a moment, but the real garden held only Lisa, sheltering under the magnolia with her hands planted in the small of her back.

'When I fell on the sand,' said Ruby, 'I felt so much pain, I thought I was dying. My insides were being ripped out. I could taste it on my tongue: salt, harsh death. I was sure the baby was gone. And I just thought – no. No, I don't want this. I want to live.'

'Why didn't you tell anyone before? About the baby, I mean?'

Ruby looked impatient. 'Lots of reasons. For a long time I wasn't sure I was pregnant. I wasn't sure I wanted to be. Then when I realised, I spoke to Valentine, and I found he was the sort of man everyone had warned me he was. And I was just the kind of fool I've always despised. Then I *couldn't* tell. I couldn't stand the looks of pity I'd get from your mother, for one. See how she's trying to take me under her wing now. The only way she can stand having Val's child around is by becoming some kind of earth-mother. I won't be part of her brood, I *won't*! That's why I've got to get away.'

'Away?' repeated Daniel, puzzled.

'Away from Morton's Holt. I've a friend in Durham. She's on her own, and she's got a kid herself. We were thinking we could help each other out. I'll be moving in with her next month.'

Daniel stared at her. 'Do Mum and Max know about this?'

'I'm going to break it to Dad this afternoon. After his do at the Exhibition Centre.'

'He won't like it,' said Daniel slowly.

'No. That's why I'll tell him nicely.'

'But Durham? I thought you were taking a year off.' The decision seemed like folly to Daniel.

'That doesn't mean I have to stay here. I'll be all right, you'll see. Besides, Dad's very keen to write me cheques at the moment. I think I'd better take them.'

'It's not that. He owes you more than he'll ever be able to pay that way. But—'

Ruby smiled. 'Have you heard him rhapsodising on the theme of grandfatherhood?'

'But what about the nappies and the feeds? Everything you said about Mum's baby? How will you deal with it?'

'Oh, I don't know, Daniel! Do you expect me to have all the answers? Celeste will help. Stop pestering me now, little brother – I want to lie in the sun.'

Ruby curled her legs up under her, and tucked her hands behind her head. Daniel smiled a little at his dismissal – smiled that he didn't mind it. An unexpected spring of good will was flowing through him, towards Ruby, Max and everyone. A new sister, a new brother too. He didn't mind. But Durham! Max would have to talk her round. He left, and went to help his mother with the weeds.

In the afternoon Max drove him to the harbour. There the local MP was due to open the new Exhibition Centre, whose logo Max had designed. The city and the sea was the centre's theme, one thousand years past and the thousand more to come. Max had placed his yin-yang dolphins on top of an anchor, with a shopping mall rampant. They fluttered on a dozen orange pennants, and were duplicated in a stone slab above the centre's main doors.

Daniel stood between the columns of the portico, and looked out at the harbour. The drizzle had ceased, leaving the stone steps sun-washed. The surface of the sea-movement against the harbour was caressing the boats, coaxing them back and forth, mirroring them to advantage. *The Cuthbert, La Belle Cecile, The Concrete Evidence* all swayed, their rhythm checked by the mooring ropes. He gazed up to the fort headland, following the white bollards till they shrank to match-heads. The fort was a boulder on the hill's crest, ready to be pitched off by the first wind. And then the violet sky beyond. A storm, out at sea. Limitless, the sea. If anything could take a human soul and beat it thin, to filmy air, to nothing ...

Timon existed below that horizon. In what form, Daniel could no more imagine than he could breathe the lightless water there. That was Necropolis, the dead's city. City of forgetting. If they met again they would not know each other. Nature would have made its anagrams of them.

A dizzying wave of sadness broke upon Daniel, a pain it would take more than time to heal. He turned his gaze landward. In the distance a crane working on the sea walls lifted another joist, a petal hung from spider's silk. Where would next year's spring tide find him?

'Hello, Daniel,' said a voice at his shoulder.

'Jane!'

Jane stood beside him, shy in a moss-green coat. 'I guessed you'd be here,' she said.

'You wanted to see me?' he asked, surprised. 'After the things I said to you?' At school, she seemed to have been avoiding him.

She nodded. 'I heard what happened. Bits of it.'

'Oh, right,' said Daniel. 'What did you hear?'

'There was something on the radio. About how you were a hero. They said your sister had fallen off the quay, and you rescued her.'

'That's true, more or less,' Daniel faltered.

'It's the "less" bit I'm interested in. Oh, don't worry, I'm not about to run off to the papers. I just need to know. Does it have anything to do with what happened to Gabriel that night?'

Daniel grimaced. 'You needn't worry, nothing like that will happen again,' he said. 'Gabriel's quite safe.'

'That's not an answer, is it? And it's not for Gabriel I'm asking. It's for myself.' Jane paused before adding: 'For you too, maybe.'

Daniel peered at her. Her eyes were quicker than he remembered, seeing and reflecting more of the sun-bright scene around them. Her mouth, its slight plumpness, and the voice that had so charmed him, now seemed less beautiful, more unhappy, kinder. Oddly, he thought of her father: the way he had looked when he had turned up at the hospital, luminous with anger; the regiments of daffodils in his garden; the venetian blinds shut. And he began to guess what had gone into her life – how hard she would need to fight to find her own way. And how much use a love-sick child would be.

'I've been a fool with you, haven't I?' he declared suddenly.

She shrugged. 'It doesn't have to be like that for ever, does it?'

'No,' agreed Daniel. 'No, why should it?'

She walked with him along the quay.

'I could tell the minute I saw you that something had changed. Even the way you stand, it shows. Like a weight's been lifted off.'

Daniel said impulsively: 'It does have to do with Gabriel. With what attacked him.'

'Yes?'

'Explaining will take time, though. I'm still explaining to myself. It's not just finding words.'

'But it's about your brother?'

Daniel nodded slowly. 'Why do you say that?'

'I'm not stupid. I've been wondering why Ruby would end up just there on the sand, of all places. And what you said about him having no face left ...'

'I don't know what's happened to Timon,' said Daniel quickly. 'Something terrible, I think.'

'But is he dead? Really dead now?'

'I don't know,' said Daniel. 'I guess I can't talk about it yet.'

'But one day you'll have to. Soon, perhaps.'

Daniel nodded, and looked back at the sky above the headland. The storm had stayed far out at sea, today. 'Then I'll be ready.'

Max's logo was unveiled on time. The MP made a speech about prosperity, and the spirit of the Merchant Venturers which, in this new Exhibition Centre, was so splendidly revived. The architect congratulated everyone. Max beamed, his world complete. And here was Ruby herself, walking towards them, newspaper in hand.

'That reminds me, where's the photographer gone?' asked Max. 'The *Post* was going to do a word or two about me. Have you seen anyone who looks the part, Daniel?'

'What have I missed?' called Ruby. She glanced up the steps to the place where Max was standing with the other dignitaries. 'Dad, when *will* you learn to do your tie properly?'

Max was not discomfited. 'You should be in this too,' he declared as the photographer arrived.

'Dad,' said Ruby seriously. 'There's something I need to talk to you about.'

'Not more revelations, darling!' pleaded Max. 'I'm not sure my frame can stand it.'

'You look pretty flexible to me. Besides, I'll buy you a drink – they'll be open at the Rummer in ten minutes.'

Max replied from the top of the step and tapped his watch, but his voice was drowned by the outcry of the gulls in the harbour, disputing a carcass. The photographer was asking him to smile.

'It's OK,' called Ruby. 'I suppose my new life plan can wait a little. You get your slice of glory.' She turned and walked back to the quayside steps where Daniel and Jane were sitting. The water pitched and dipped and broke at their feet. Daniel, half-enchanted, hardly noticed as she sat beside him. But he heard her murmur to the petty waves: 'Then swallow hard, dear Dad, and take a seat. I think you're going to need it.'

Also by Charles Butler

The Darkling

"*The Darkling's mouth flapped open at the jaw, and a slow stream of spittle snaked towards the table. I ran for the door.*"

Since childhood, 15-year-old Petra has loved to scare herself with the Darkling, a make-believe creature made of night-time shadows. But what happens when the Darkling takes on a life of its own? What happens when he reveals the tragic secret of Century Hall and its sinister owner?

No one, not even Petra, could imagine the terrifying events that will be unleashed and change her life forever.

"A brilliant first book, Mr Butler!"

School Librarian